7

# WICKED BLOOD

## SAM WICK UNIVERSE THRILLER #7

### CHASE AUSTIN

THRILLVERSE PUBLISHING

# ABOUT WICKED BLOOD

*America is under attack and the world's most powerful nation isn't the least bit ready for it.* **Can Sam Wick save his motherland?**

**Sam Wick** is Task Force 77's best. Master Extractor. Perfect Assassin. Where the government cannot and will not go, he will.

Task Force-77 (TF-77) is a black ops team of NSA and the US Military. This is the team the U.S. government calls when it needs to get people out of the most dangerous places on earth.

What Readers are saying about Sam Wick's Adventures;

---

★★★★★ "One heck of an entertaining and intense ride... Fast, entertaining, suspenseful and action-packed... you will find yourself flying through and it will be hard to let it go!" - Amazon Review

★★★★★ "Fast paced read with a Kick-Ass hero you can't help rooting for." - Amazon Review

★★★★★ "Full of awesome action. I can't wait to read the next book" - Amazon Review

★★★★★ " I did not put this book down for any reason other than to eat." - Amazon Review

★★★★★ "Fast paced, lots of thrills. Highly entertaining." - Amazon Review

★★★★★ "I'm ready for Sam's next assignment." - Amazon Review

PART 1

# CHAPTER 1

ZANGABAD, **Afghanistan**

The unnamed shooter, code named 'Z', was glued to his glass, scrutinizing the vast terrain that lay in front of him. His target was a sniper named Eddie, a short and wiry El Paso stock with a boyish grin, black hair, and vital green eyes, lying on his belly and covered with foliage, some hundred yards away.

Eddie was part of an elite black ops team - Task Force 77 - jointly overseen by the NSA and the US military. It was created to execute the toughest missions, penetrate the most dangerous locations, often through means that no government could overtly authorize. Except for a handful of individuals, no one (not even the President of the US) knew the exact size of this team or how many assets it had.

. . .

Eddie was one of TF-77's best snipers. Right then he had no idea that while he was finding his targets, he was in the crosshairs of someone else's weapon. It would be the easiest of his predator's kills, but the shooter wasn't there to assassinate him. His orders were clear. His client wanted him to make sure that the sniper and his partner, Sam Wick, finished their mission successfully.

Eddie's partner - Sam Wick, who at the moment was hiding in plain sight some sixteen hundred yards away and closer to Eddie's targets - was widely considered to be the best among the current crop of TF-77 assets. With a hit rate of ninety-five percent for the last five years, he had rarely come back without results from his missions. He stood 5'11 and his weather-beaten face had a rugged attraction, not least because of his unreadable sea-blue eyes, bright with intelligence. With his slicked-back black hair and athletic build, he seemed like a man always on a mission. His looks, and his ability to speak seventeen languages with a neutral accent, including Arabic, Urdu, and Hindi, made him an excellent choice for deployment in countries like Afghanistan, Iraq, and Pakistan. He considered himself to be an orphan, that is, until seven months ago, when during a mission in Poland, he stumbled onto some key information about his parents and the possibility that they might still be alive. Someone called 'Professor' was the key to this puzzle, but so far, he had been unsuccessful in finding anything substantial about his parents, or about this faceless man.

For the last few months, Sam had been stationed in Afghanistan, tailing Abdul Basit, a Taliban commander.

.  .  .

Z knew everything he needed to know about Wick and Eddie because of the one page brief about given to him about his targets by his client. He knew that they were Americans, but why they were here, he had no idea. For Z it was an opportunity where the task was simple and the payout, huge. Easiest money ever made.

He had tailed Eddie and Wick from the city using a tracking device glued to the belly of the Ford in which the duo were traveling. He watched them separate at the edge of Zangabad, with Eddie taking the Ford to the foot of a desolate hill with a better vantage point of his target. Z instinctively followed the Ford.

Lying on his belly, Z checked Eddie's position and then the position of his target from the glass. The target was a single wooden door in the middle of a vast territory, roughly sixteen hundred yards away. It was too far even for Z's own comfort.

Would Eddie be able to take the shot? Z didn't know but he would soon.

Eddie repositioned himself. Facing North, bleeding sweat, he lowered his eye to the glass, aiming towards the door. Crosshairs tracked to a distant one-room set. Sixteen hundred yards out. Everything was fumes.

His crosshairs tracked back, measuring, calculating the distance. He was back on target.

Z, a hundred yards behind Eddie, watched with interest. It was an impossible shot, almost.

Eddie's crosshairs wobbled on the first dark shape. He muttered to himself, *'Aim small. Aim fucking small'*.

He could not see the obscured face, only a black mass. A prayer susurrated from his dry lips. He fired.

The shooter followed the shot through his own glass. The shot echoed for eternity. Seconds later, a red mist painted the hut's wall.

The shooter felt an unknown elation and a touch of jealousy. "Shit," he muttered under his breath. He had just seen Eddie - one of the best in the sniping business - get a 10 on 10 shot, and move on to the next target without wasting time.

. . .

Z saw another man going down.

Z then saw Wick in the distance, sprinting. A Beretta in his hand. His shooting hand rose in the air and the bullets pierced the last surviving man. The three men didn't even get a chance to properly lift their weapons.

Wick vanished inside the door and now both Eddie and the shooter could only wait. Some twenty minutes later, Wick emerged from the door carrying a wounded body.

Wick ambled towards the open Toyota and put the injured man on the front passenger seat. He then vanished behind the door, again. Z quickly fetched a expensive camera from his bag. He had to take some photos as proof.

Five minutes later, Wick reappeared at the door with another body. Running towards the open SUV, he put the body on the back seat and then ran back to the hut again. The third time when he reappeared, he took control of the SUV and the four-wheeler finally accelerated. Z soon realized the reason for his hurry. With the first blast that rocked the terrain, the one-room hut had started to crumple to the ground. The earth began shaking and the ground had started to vanish in an unending pit.

. . .

Z kept on taking pictures in rapid succession, documenting everything.

From the corner of his eye, Z saw Eddie gathering his things and he slowly crawled back to hide himself. Soon, the engine growled, and the SUV lurched forward. Z didn't follow Eddie but remained at his place, watching the trail of dust left by the Ford. He just kept on clicking pictures.

As both Wick and Eddie raced away to get out of the sight, Z opened his bag and took out a satellite phone. The call was answered on the second ring, as if the man on the other side was waiting for him.

"They have saved two men and bombed the bunker," Z reported.

"What about you?"

"They don't know about me."

"Send me pictures," the man ordered.

# CHAPTER 2

## THE LOUVRE MUSEUM, Paris.

The man was among the many who stood gazing at the naked woman. His flight had landed at the Paris Charles de Gaulle Airport that morning. As an American visiting Paris for pleasure, the first thing he went to do was to see Jean Auguste Dominique Ingres' Grand Odalisque at the Louvre. He liked the Mona Lisas and the Venus de Milos of the world, but nothing gave him the peace he always sought, as the Grand Odalisque did. It was a figure depicting a young woman supposedly living in the harem of an Eastern Sultan. The painting brimmed with exoticism, eroticism, and the sort of sexual availability that the women of Western Europe were thought not to possess. It was a striking study of female beauty and at the same time an illustration of male desire warping the image of women.

· · ·

His heterochromatic eyes, the blue left eye and green right eye, were hidden behind a pair of Gucci blue-rimmed sunglasses. A gold earring pierced in his right earlobe. He looked sharp and alert in a bespoke three-piece suit, but that facade of sophistication hid a serpent that not even his closest confidante knew about. Standing in the thin crowd, he checked his Rolex, still set to US time zone. The culmination of years of hard work was finally coming to a closure today.

No one knew how he had looked when he was twenty, thirty or forty. His face had undergone multiple plastic surgeries over the years, so much so that he himself barely recollected how he may have looked in the beginning. He didn't even think of it anymore.

Rumor had it that he was once an undercover agent and assassin for hire for one of the USA agencies. Prior to that he probably worked as an informant for the Drug Enforcement Agency (DEA) and then as a vital asset for the CIA and NSA, and at some point, he came in contact with either ISIS or Al Qaeda where he became their best soldier. But no one knew the truth or his real identity. From the time he came in this profession, he had always lived with aliases and cover. His current alias was 'The Professor' and he was fine with it as long as he got what he wanted. And right now, he only wanted one thing–annihilation of a nation that had betrayed him and his loyalty.

The Professor opened the image gallery on his cell phone and looked at a picture. Sam Wick was standing on the verge of the burned police station in Helmand, Afghanistan. The next image was of Wick driving an open Toyota while the blast rocked the terrain behind him.

*'Kid, you are doing exactly what I want you to.'* He smiled.

He swiped right with his thumb. The next image was a monochrome one – of William Helms, the director of NSA and the custodian of TF-77 - having dinner with his wife and daughter at his home.

*'Now let's see what you can do.'* He smiled again.

⸻

The plan had been set in motion two years ago. He and his small team of assassins, hackers, strategists, and political pawns had spent the major part of their lives in several cities in the USA, studying them as no one ever had. No one knew that until just before the plot started to take shape, he had been called Masood Akram – half Iraqi and half American. It was another of his aliases helping ISIS to keep their flags high. That mission had been a job meant for a lone wolf, and he had completed it with perfection. But for this mission, he needed people who were not afraid to kill or be killed.

.  .  .

His first recruit was a cleric in Pakistan, Irfan-Ul-Haq, AKA The Cleric, whose job was to use every tactic in the book to route American aid to the ones who would not hesitate to kill and die.

His next hire was Ed McCarthy, AKA Yasin Malik, an American who had converted to Islam from Christianity. His job was to hire and train the recruits using the money arranged by The Cleric.

The third piece of the puzzle was to get the weapons and explosives deliver to the target locations, which his team had taken care of.

During all this, in one of his visits to Paris he had met Fleur – a breathtaking French beauty and an art curator by profession. For her, he was an independent filmmaker. Sparks flew between the two and before anyone could say *what*, they were married. The following month, he and Fleur arrived at Houston and stayed at the Onyx – a 7-Star hotel at the Marina – Houston's biggest mall. For her it was an amazing honeymoon, for him it was a chance to recce the hotel which was one of the targets. He filmed elaborate videos of Fleur on the pretext of his love for her, but the aim was to capture the moving images of the hotel and its security.

The GPS waypoints and videos were the means to train people to navigate the buildings like pros despite the fact that they had never ventured out of their small towns and cities into hotels like this one. He knew that the city police or the SWAT teams could not withstand a military-style assault. He and his team planned everything with a huge amount of research and deep site recces and now it had to be carried out with clockwork precision to be effective.

For the last two weeks, everything had been coming together at breakneck speed, but something was amiss. There was no fun! The intelligence agencies had no inkling about the attack, which wasn't surprising, but the Professor wanted them to know and act and then fail in their attempts. That would be real entertainment. They would squirm and wiggle and yet submit to his will and planning. That would be the real victory.

When he got the intel about someone named Abdul Basit capturing a CIA agent in Afghanistan, his brain started to work overtime. According to his sources, Basit worked for Irfan-Ul-Haq, the Cleric from Pakistan who was working for him. That piece of information gave him an idea. Using his sources, he decided to relay the intel to the CIA, hoping that they would at least try to save their agent... and then they would get the information about the planned attack, which he wanted to happen. But then the CIA director, Walter Raborn, had done something entirely unexpected! He involved TF-77. It was a startling move, yet even the Professor could not have thought of a better way to inject more excitement in the proceedings. From the time he heard of TF-77's involvement, he activated one of his contractors, Z, to keep an eye on Wick and Eddie, only to make sure that they completed their mission and got the information about the impending attack.

Now that their mission was a success, he just had to wait for the American bureaucracy to start moving at its glacial pace to stop the attacks, while he stood appreciating the exquisiteness of Paris and Jean Auguste Dominique Ingres' paintings. He had made sure that the country that betrayed him would witness something that no one ever thought possible. And he would relish every moment of it from the comfort of his hotel room on a 50-inch television set.

# CHAPTER 3

"You've sinned, Mahfouz." Yasin Malik's voice reverberated in the abandoned hangar. Standing on a platform, Yasin looked down on a 19-year-old young man. The man was Otis but in the camp people knew him as Mahfouz, and Mahfouz was on trial for his sins. "You've violated the sacred pact between yourself and Allah. You have betrayed your brothers. You've broken their trust, but Allah is kind. He wants you to choose your own destiny. So, what will it be, Mahfouz? What's your destiny?" Yasin's black eyes gazed at the impressionable young man.

"I deserve death."

. . .

Twenty-nine other young men in three straight lines watched Mahfouz choosing his destiny with a certain defiance.

"Speak to everyone about your sin." Yasin was the judge but the twenty-nine others were the jury.

"I broke the sacred pact when I asked one of my brothers about his family. The family that we have forsaken."

"Mahfouz, why did you do that?" Yasin's voice was pained.

Mahfouz remained silent.

Yasin looked at the sky and closed his eyes. "Inna lillahi wa inna ilayhi raji'un. (We belong to Allah, and to Him we shall return)." He opened his eyes and observed his students.

He spoke with finality. "Your time has come." Twenty-nine pairs of feet moved towards Mahfouz.

Mahfouz turned to face his executioners. In their eyes he could see a multitude of emotions — hate, fear, shock, rejection and...sympathy.

.    .    .

"Don't worry, Allah will be kind," Mahfouz spoke to his executioners. These boys were his brothers, and he wanted them to be strong.

Shahrukh, who was closest to Mahfouz, dealt the first blow. Mahfouz saw it coming and his natural instincts forced him to block it with both hands.

"Forgive me." The two words immediately escaped his lips.

The first blow was the initiation. Then body blows and kicks rained on him. He took them all without putting up a defense. But his young, vulnerable body could only take so much. He fell to the ground, but none of his executioners stopped.

Yasin remained on the platform watching Mahfouz being trampled to death. His pupils had just passed the last stage of their six-month-long training magnificently. He now had twenty-nine merciless, trained soldiers who would do anything he wanted them to do. And today he wanted America to burn.

# CHAPTER 4

YASIN MALIK WAS in his private room, sitting on his knees, his hands placed flat on his thighs. "O Allah, forgive me, have mercy on me, strengthen me, raise me in status, pardon me and grant me the provision," he murmured.

Shahrukh, a twenty-year-old young man and one of his star pupils, stood silently at the open door, waiting for Yasin to notice him. His eyes were alert, posture tense, gaze fixed on his commander. He didn't dare interrupt Yasin during his *Namaz*. No one did.

"Subhanna rabbiyal a'laa. Subhanna rabbiyal a'laa. Subhanna rabbiyal a'laa." Yasin turned his head, first to his right and then left. He opened his eyes unhurriedly and noticed Shahrukh at the door, watching his every move like a loyal servant.

. . .

Yasin got to his feet and put on his shoes. He gave Shahrukh a nod to let him know he was ready. Shahrukh nodded in return and turned around to alert the others.

Yasin smiled to himself, thinking of the fidelity Shahrukh and others had towards his words. From the day this had begun, Yasin had vigorously sought boys like Shahrukh to be part of his army. They were loyal to the core and highly impressionable. What they lacked was training, and Yasin had polished them, to be both effective and efficient. Each one of them. Thirty in total. Now twenty-nine. Ready to plunge into anything with everything they had, at Yasin's word.

Now was the time to test their mettle.

Yasin replaced his kufi skullcap, worn during the Namaz, with a white Islamic turban. Military green fatigues completed the rest of his getup.

⊏⊐

Yasin had set up the training facility in the hangar of a deserted airfield, in the Texas boondocks where there was no hum of traffic or buzz of streetlights. Just crickets. Companions Yasin didn't mind. In fact, 'hangar' was a very loose description of the space. It was more like a warehouse — high ceiling, cracked floor, rust eating away at the walls. The roller doors were up, and the entire structure seemed like it wouldn't take more than a slight breeze to collapse it.

The building was illuminated with flickering overhead lights. Outside, overgrown weeds snaked through the cracks. A field of dead grass stretched out in all directions revealing nothing but flat ground as far as the eye could see. But there was something else. Three Bell 205As and three Cessnas sat outside, ready for take-off.

The air was lighter compared to the heaviness of the city, but it was still hot and wet. The night breeze failed to give any respite. Yasin sweltered in the heat, but he had seen worse. He paid scant attention to it as he walked towards his mentees waiting for him in three straight lines next to a makeshift platform at the far corner of the hangar, the very place from where he had sentenced Mahfouz to death.

# CHAPTER 5

THE CADETS BOWED their heads as Yasin walked up to the dais. He turned to face twenty-nine pair of eyes. His sleeves were rolled up, revealing muscular forearms. His face was thoughtful and intelligent, but it betrayed no emotion. A warrior's look was in his eyes. They all recognized the intensity — a mix of determination and ruthlessness.

To strangers, he appeared as normal as one would expect a person to be. He had a full head of thick black hair and a tanned face with a trimmed beard and a sharp mustache. People knew him as Ed McCarthy, a mild-mannered security guard at this deserted airfield, employed by an obscure North Dakota facilities management firm. On paper, his job was to take care of the airstrip and the hangar. The nearest town was fifteen miles to the north, and he rarely visited it. Whenever he did, it was always for groceries, which were always paid for in cash. The cashier never looked at him twice. No one ever did.

. . .

Seven months ago, Yasin had appeared in this town with three men. For the next thirty days they had worked on creating makeshift living spaces for thirty more people, a soundproof space that covered one-third of the hangar, a simulation room, and a makeshift kitchen. All this required cash. The money had found its way to him through Irfan-Ul-Haq, AKA the Great Cleric.

On the thirty-first day, the three men had left, leaving Yasin alone. Two days later, the first lot of fifteen men arrived and three days later, the next fifteen. And for the next six months they lived on that airfield, right under the American government's nose, plotting the country's downfall. Getting trained in hand-to-hand combat, the use of different kinds of firearms — assault rifles, submachine guns, and pistols — in the soundproof cabins. They learned to handle grenades and worked with every known kind of explosive. The training also covered a detailed lowdown of guerilla warfare and the deadly Palestinian terror strategies of deep insertion. At the end of six months, Yasin had converted them into live ammunition, using the Taliban's playbook.

At times Yasin found the process of turning a misguided American kid into a walking time-bomb bloody hard. He felt as if he would never succeed, or someday a SWAT team would raid the compound and take him and his whole operation down, but he persisted. He persisted, and persisted, in the name of Allah.

. . .

The training was regimented. The whole process of breaking and molding young distressed minds was divided into six major steps.

Step one was to prey on kids from dysfunctional or broken families; isolate them from their parents and their familiar surroundings. The kids were selected based on their age, mixed parentage and citizenship. They were young, had one Muslim parent and were American citizens with valid social security numbers. Some of them were from affluent families, several had parents who commanded wide respect in their communities, almost all had gone to good schools and been at the top of their class for most of their academic lives. But the most important thing they had in common was their extreme loathing for society.

Step two started with the teaching of Koran, Islam's holiest book, in Arabic, a language these youngsters didn't understand and couldn't speak. This made them rely heavily on Yasin, who then distorted the message as and when it suited his purpose. The trainees were explicitly forbidden to contact their families, read newspapers, listen to radio, read any books that Yasin did not prescribe for them, thus creating a complete blackout. The cadets were given a new identity. None of them could ask anyone else about anything except what they were learning there. Talking about old identities or families or girlfriends or past life was forbidden; breaking this pact meant a death sentence. The mission was more important than small talk about one's past.

.   .   .

The third step was to make these young men hate the world that they currently lived in. Every single day for eight hours all they had to do was to read the Koran. Many a day they were beaten, fed only dry bread and water.

The next step was to drill the concept of martyrdom glories. How when they would die, they would be received up with unimaginable pleasures and food, and how this glory was going to propel them to become heroes in their neighborhoods.

The penultimate step was to show them videos of how minorities were being treated in the USA, how men, women, and children were suffering and dying at the hands of the American administration and how American politicians were milking the country dry, letting the nation go to the dogs. The underlying message was that modern America didn't care about their own and others, so those who supported the government deserved to die. At the end of these phases, the youngsters were ready to go out and fight because that was the only way to eternal glory.

The last stage of the training was to assess if they would hesitate to kill a fellow American, and that was why, even though Yasin came to know about Mahfouz's breach of trust very early, he still waited till the last day of the training to sentence him to death at the hands of his mates. By sacrificing Mahfouz, he had made sure that his six months of regimented training was successful in weeding out any vestige of humanity from every cadet's consciousness. Now, not a shred of emotion or doubt would cloud their minds when the time came for them to kill.

Out of the thirty, Yasin had also chosen five to execute five unique jobs. Their given names were Taha, Habib, Sultan, Rahim, and Aslam. Their real names were Liam, Ethan, Mason, William, and Elijah, but not anymore. They were the youngest in the lot, from fourteen to seventeen years of age. Unlike the rest of the trainees on that airfield, these five were different and were treated differently. Yasin wanted more like them but soon found out that only those five had the right psyche and that they fit the criteria to a tee. Now, Yasin's only job was to nurture them to be the best.

The target cities and the buildings had already been identified, code-named and broken down to their bare basics — subways, police station locations, sewer networks, train systems, electric grids, water supplies, government institutions, schools, malls, theaters. Weekly simulations augmented familiarity with the terrain. Mock battles in which different ground situations were replicated gave the young men a real feel of covering their bases quickly while taking care of any obstructions.

Still, Yasin knew that no training could prepare them to take on the FBI and the CIA, and that's why the attacks were not aimed to seize control but to inflict maximum damage, and then immediately withdraw to avoid retaliation. The assault's sole objective was 'destroy and move'.

.   .   .

America wouldn't even know what hit her.

# CHAPTER 6

YASIN CLENCHED his right wrist with his left hand, behind his back. His posture was erect and attentive, his gaze fixed on the twenty-nine men standing before him in silence. His lips quivered and slowly the words started to take the shape of a speech. He had practiced it a zillion times in the privacy of his room, but tonight was the real test for him. This was the last thing his men were going to take with them.

"Allah has created us for his worship and commanded us to be just, and allowed us, the wronged ones, to retaliate against our oppressor." His words came out in a measured tone. "Today we are gathered here to commence the most pious mission bestowed on us by Him, that is, to avenge the deaths of millions of our brothers and sisters at the hands of this barbaric nation – America – and fix its broken system. Today marks the beginning of a new order where idiots will not occupy the top places. They will not tell us how to live our lives. This nation and its leadership must realize that every human life has the same value. It must realize that we have suffered enough, and we are done being at the wrong end of their bullets, bombs, and missiles. Today the bullets, bombs, and missiles will have new targets. The assailant will become the prey."

Yasin paused to gauge his audience. They all were listening with rapt attention. "Our brothers and sisters are being killed and terrorized by America, within the borders and outside of them, and our brethren want us to do something. Today we'll make them proud. We'll teach this cruel nation a lesson on how to treat human life justly. America is our home too and a man cannot be blamed for protecting his home. This American system is beyond repair. Its hands are tainted with the blood of innocents and it's time to return the favor in kind." Yasin was almost at the conclusion of his speech. He could see the boys were charged up. It was time to give them one last push. "Allahu Akbar."

"Allahu Akbar." The boys shouted back.

"We are ready." Yasin raised his right hand in the air.

"Ready to kill." Twenty-nine right hands were up in solidarity. For the next few seconds, no one said anything. They just gazed at each other.

Yasin stared hard at the three men who would be leading the three teams in the battlefield. Khalid Sheikh Mohammed, Shahrukh Umar, and Saif al-Adel were standing there, leading the three rows. Six months ago, they had names like Max, Jacob, and Pete but now they were Khalid Sheikh Mohammed, Shahrukh Umar, and Saif al-Adel. Others were instructed to follow these three on the battlefield because Yasin wasn't going to be there. He had other things to take care of, like dismantling this facility so that when the uniforms came sniffing, they would find nothing.

Yasin knew that none of the twenty-nine mentees was going to come out of this mission alive. He had made sure of that. There wasn't any escape plan. Surrender wasn't even an option. Once they were in, they had only two options – Kill or Die.

He slowly got off the podium and strutted towards Khalid, the nearest of the three. "I have very high hopes for you," he said.

"Yes, Commander." There was pride in Khalid's answer. Yasin's smile in return was that of a proud father. Khalid's actual father was the vice president of one of the American oil and gas majors and his mother was marketing director in an Internet unicorn startup. They had no idea that their son, whom they thought was in his college dorm room, and right then probably asleep, was, in fact, getting ready to wage a war against his own country. They would, however, know it all too soon.

Yasin then paused near Saif and widened his hands for a hug, which Saif gladly accepted. He said, "Saif, make me proud."

"Yes, Commander," Saif spoke in Yasin's ear. Saif's actual father was a USA district judge and his mother an elementary school teacher. Their son, according to them, was on a foreign trip to Italy sponsored by his college. They had spoken to him only twice in the last six months despite the multiple options the world now had in terms of reaching out to people.

Shahrukh was last in the line. His father, a successful investment banker and his mother, an award-winning journalist, had been on the road for the last nine months for work commitments and believed that their academically bright son was at their home busy preparing for Harvard.

Yasin said to Shahrukh, "You are my pride, my Simba. Ask for anything?"

"You have shown us the right path, what else can I ask for?" Shahrukh was sincere and completely in awe of his master. By the end of the sentence, his voice choked with emotions. Yasin patted his right shoulder and smiled.

·  ·  ·

He took a step back from the cadets. "May Allah be with you all," he wished them loudly.

"Allah is always with us," his boys responded.

One by one Yasin met the rest, looked them in the eye, and wished them success.

Some of them turned emotional. *How could they ever repay him?*

They had to make Yasin proud of their sacrifices.

# CHAPTER 7

"IT'S TIME," Yasin said, glancing at his watch. On his command, the squad walked to the helis. The pilots were alert and the gates of the Bells already open. The men gazed at Yasin one last time and started boarding. Twenty-four men in three teams of eight boarded the three Bells. Taha, Habib, Sultan, Rahim, and Aslam stayed back with Yasin.

Yasin signaled the pilots once the three teams were on board, and the birds took off. Once the last Bell left the ground, Yasin gazed with pride at the special five men with him. "Allah loves you more than your brothers," he said. "That's why he has chosen you for this unique mission."

"Allah is kind." They all spoke in unison.

Yasin, looking at the five of them, felt extremely proud of his creations. He gestured at the three Cessnas. Taha and

Habib walked towards the first one, Sultan and Aslam towards the second, and Rahim went for the last one. The pilots were already at their seats. Once the three Cessna were airborne, Yasin turned and walked towards his private room. In the room, he shifted the wooden wall using a lever. There was a small 3X5 steel locker. He keyed in the pass-code to open it. Inside there was a satellite phone. Taking out the satellite phone, he plugged in the numbers from memory. The phone on the other side was picked on the fourth ring.

"As-Salaam-Alaikum, Janaab," Yasin greeted the receiver.

"Alaykum as-salām, Yasin." The receiver was the Great Cleric, whose somber voice was reassuring.

"The birds are in motion and will reach their destination before the sun rises today."

"Eamal jayid."

"Shukriya, Janaab."

"Goodbye, Yasin."

. . .

"Good…" the line was disconnected even before Yasin could finish his goodbye, but he didn't have time to dwell on it. It was time for him to vanish because he needed to live to find more sacrificial lambs for this war because this war wasn't over yet.

———

Irfan-Ul-Haq AKA Great Cleric turned to watch the silhouette on the screen.

"So, we are on time." The silhouette spoke in a measured tone. His modulated computerized voice echoed in the room through two tiny speakers.

"Yes, sir," the Cleric responded with respect clothed in fear. He had no idea who the other man was or even what he looked like. All he had was a name, 'Professor', which was probably a facade too. The only thing that interested him was that the man seemed to have unlimited resources at his disposal, which Irfan eyed. Even though the Cleric was getting a good deal of money once this mission was done, there remained a sense of unease still. The noose around his neck could be tightened any minute if the Professor decided, and the Cleric could do nothing. He was beset with insecurities he could not define.

On the other hand, there was nothing about the Great Cleric that wasn't known to the Professor. He knew all about his illegal bank accounts, his dealings with the Pakistan's Inter-Service Intelligence (ISI) and the Taliban, even his human trafficking business.

The Professor spoke in measured tones, "You know what you have to do?"

"Yes, sir."

"I will not disturb you and your men now. Your money will be in your account once we cross the forty-eight-hour timeline from the time the mission starts."

"Thank you, sir." Irfan gave a feeble smile, but the screen had already gone black.

The Cleric's payment had always reached him on time. But this time it was different, this was the last leg of the mission and he knew the man would vanish once this was over. *What if he decided not to pay him? What would he do then? But if the man did, then forty-eight hours later the Great Cleric would be one of the richest men in Pakistan.*

The Cleric didn't know what to do with these contradictory thoughts. He could only hope that his luck wouldn't desert him now.

# CHAPTER 8

The farmland stretched as far as one could see and in the middle of it, a square-shaped helipad was illuminated with incandescent lights at its edges. The area was guarded by four gunners; their faces covered with black masks. Five similar teams were on alert in the other five target cities.

The Bell's pilot checked the weather and the dashboard. The coast was clear for landing. He announced on the microphone to let the passengers know about it. Shahrukh heard the announcement and watched Yakub, who was sitting diagonally to him. His eyes were alert, but his face was blank. Shahrukh figured that his own expression might be similar. He shifted his gaze to the window. The sun was about to rise. The dawn was breathing its last.

. . .

The Bell circled the landing spot, checking for obstacles, planning its approach. Once the pilot was satisfied, he brought down the speed gradually, careful not to overshoot the landing site. The bird hovered just above the square-shaped location, but the pilot knew it wasn't a rush job. Despite the perception that a helicopter could land anywhere, and only needed a small square to land, it was a difficult beast to control, especially in confined or uneven spaces like farmlands.

The pilot's primary concern was not to get into a vortex ring, which simply meant an uncontrolled descent of the helicopter falling into its own downwash and killing everyone. The bird had to gradually descend vertically. The Bell steadied and then touched the ground but not before shaking one last time. The door opened only when the rotors started to cool off. The eight young men disembarked the plane, walking in a line, and instantly felt a shiver due to the icy breeze emanating from the rotors.

The four gunners instinctively closed in on them but stopped at a comfortable distance. They let Shahrukh and his team cover the rest of the distance after disembarking. One of the gunners, who seemed to be the leader, came forward two steps and lifted his right hand to his forehead in a slicing motion. "As-Salam-u-Alaikum."

"Wa-Alaikumussalam wa-Rahmatullah," said Shahrukh, responding with the same gesture.

· · ·

"How was the journey?" the leader asked.

"Good," Shahrukh smiled.

The leader gestured at two of his gunners and said, "They will take you to your destination."

The two gunmen assigned to escort the squad led the path to the two SUVs parked not far from the helipad. Shahrukh and his team walked behind them, flanked by the leader and one more gunman.

The Bell's rotors had started again. It had to return to the base.

Right before boarding the SUV, Shahrukh and his men heard a suppressed gunshot followed by the sound of frightened birds leaving their nests.

"What's that sound?" Yakub seemed perturbed.

"Nothing worth worrying about," said the leader, smiling at them. "Please..." he said, and signaled Yakub to get inside. Two gunmen took the driver seats of the two SUVs and the tires started to roll on the muddy roads.

.  .  .

The leader and the gunman who stayed behind with him watched the vehicles disappearing. The leader took out his phone and dialed Yasin's number. He said, "The bird is in the air and the kids are on their way to school."

"Clean the house and move." The call was disconnected.

The leader saw his fifth colleague arriving from the country house. "The body?" he asked.

"Taken care of." The man was talking about the farm's owner.

"Good. We have one hour to take care of things here," said the leader.

# CHAPTER 9

MARYLAND, **USA**

The morning was not going as Helms had planned. He gazed at the multiple wall clocks showing times of different geographies. It was ten in the morning in Maryland but seven-thirty pm in Helmand, Afghanistan, where Wick and Eddie were on a mission.

Helms had not had a chance to sleep last night. It had all started with a call from Walter Raborn, Director of the CIA, about one of his abducted operatives. What he didn't realize was that the call was just the beginning of something he'd never expected from someone like Raborn, for two hours later he was facing the President. A meeting that was orchestrated by Raborn.

.   .   .

For the first time in his thirty-five year career, Helms wasn't ready, and he didn't know how to respond to President Hancock when he ordered, "Either you find me that abducted agent or quit." Those were his only options.

The mission was a deathtrap. The Taliban had kept the man at one of their most secure locations – Zangabad in Afghanistan, a place that had been a graveyard of the NATO forces in the past. No soldier or agent in his right mind would agree to go in there, but Helms had just demanded his men to do the impossible.

And for the first time in his life he had no answer when Wick and Eddie asked him, "What about our lives? Are they not worth saving?"

And for the first time in Helms' life, he had to ask his agents to back out if they wanted. There was no way he could tell them to continue with the mission.

Wick and Eddie eventually decided to stay on the hunt. Part of it was madness and part of it was a mad rage. It was their way of saying, fuck the politics and the politicians, we will save one of ours even if we have to sacrifice ourselves.

And now, after several hours of radio silence, Helms was on a call with Wick and Eddie. And he was listening to Wick with rapt attention. While he was happy that his assets and

Josh were breathing, the intel on rogue CIA agents was alarming. But the most pressing concern was the impending attack on the USA. No one knew the time or the exact place. They only had a vague idea, which was worth nothing, because they could not plan anything concrete based on it.

"How many bombs are we talking about?" Helms asked.

"Basit didn't know, but I don't trust him. We need more time to grill him," answered Wick.

"Why can't we go and extract the Cleric?" Eddie asked.

"That won't matter for now. If what Basit is saying is correct, then our immediate priority is to contain the attacks and minimize causalities." Wick said.

"How much damage?" asked Helms.

"That's contingent on whether we're looking at an airburst or ground detonation, and how many cities. Also, if it's detonated during the middle of the day or in the evening. Immediate casualties could be in the thousands," Wick said.

·  ·  ·

An uncomfortable silence fell over the group as everyone grappled with the enormity of the possible carnage. Eddie uttered a soft curse.

"We don't even know the type of bombs," Helms said. "My team is notifying the FBI and CIA."

"Any response from them yet?"

"FBI—yes. CIA—no, as of now," Helms said.

"Dammit," Wick muttered.

"What do you want us to do?" Eddie asked.

"Get Josh to the army medical facility in Helmand. Get Basit here. We need to interrogate him further. I'll arrange a plane for you at the airbase. Let me talk to the President." Helms said.

"I hope he doesn't do something stupid," Eddie muttered just before the line was disconnected.

# CHAPTER 10

PRESIDENT HANCOCK'S Cadillac-One sped towards his favorite golf course where he'd planned a few rounds of the game with his North Korean counterpart.

Hancock, like the USA's former president Woodrow Wilson also saw golf as a diversion from the long, high-pressured days of his job. "Each stroke requires your whole attention and seems the most important thing in life," Wilson had once said, and Hancock couldn't agree more. But his golf course visits were under intense scrutiny from media houses all over the globe.

But that wasn't all. His North Korea strategy, full of boasting and bluster, far different from that of his predecessors, was not yielding many results either. Still, supporters of his outreach cited North Korea's tension-easing suspension of nuclear and missile tests as an important step forward. But this view was a minority one in the polarized world of Washington.

Hancock's foes — and some political hawks — saw dangerous signs of a president without much grasp of foreign policy who could be played by North Korea. Even Hancock's own intelligence chief had testified last week that the North Korean Supreme Leader wasn't likely to give up his nuclear weapons.

More suspicions arose when in advance of the initial talks, Hancock had flattered and cajoled North Korea and described it as an 'economic powerhouse' in waiting, and — to the surprise of many — said he was in 'no rush' to find a deal that would dismantle its nuclear program.

Even the definition of 'denuclearization' hadn't been hammered out between U.S. and North Korean negotiators — with the North Korean regime indicating that it could entail a significant rollback of U.S. defense arrangements with allies in the region.

But this wasn't all. Midterm elections were approaching and with his latest weekly approval ratings languishing at thirty-five percent, far below that of his predecessors, his and his party's chances were not looking very bright.

. . .

Cadillac-One had one more passenger, his election campaign lead and now his Special Advisor, Peter Jackson. As the motorcade of Secret Service vehicles raced through D.C.'s concrete jungle, Jackson slowly and deliberately laid out their strategy to arrest the slide. Jackson, the Harvard Law grad and Pennsylvania native, while going through the plan one last time, ran a hand through his signature bleach-blond hair every five minutes. Hancock found it annoying but chose to ignore it. This man was majorly responsible for getting him *his* current position as US President and he still trusted him.

"This crisis presents us with a unique opportunity." Jackson started his monologue with a deliberate positive spin of the proceedings and then looked at Hancock. "People right now see you as someone who doesn't know what he is doing." He paused for effect and saw Hancock stifling his urge to counter this point. Jackson was a data guy and his every decision was based on numbers and statistics. So what he was saying now was not something out of a hat and Hancock knew that arguing with him could only result in losing the argument. And even if he won the argument, he would lose the war. Like every other time, he decided to hear where Jackson was going with this.

"This makes you the underdog and we need to make this your campaign's strength. We need to let the country know that you are in charge, and a few of your detractors are unhappy with your rise and your vision of taking America to heights of greatness again."

· · ·

"How?" Hancock blurted out, for although he didn't want to sound stupid or too eager, his words betrayed his intentions.

"You have to fire a few people from your administration. I've prepared a list," Jackson gestured at his laptop's screen.

Hancock checked the names and then looked at Jackson. A few of the names were of people he had recently praised through his social media account or had recently appointed. Firing them would lead to multiple questions about his own decisions.

"Why is this necessary?" he asked.

"I've spoken to a few publishing houses. They are interested in an insider view of the White House under your leadership." Jackson gave him the reason.

"Are you insane? Firing them and then asking them if they would be interested in writing a memoir about their life in the White House?"

Jackson had his points ready. "A disgruntled employee is as believable as life on Mars. People will talk about the books, media will have a field day, but I'll make sure you emerge victorious like a true underdog. Short term pain is always good for long-term gain." Jackson spoke with glee. "This is the idea that will win you midterms."

"Jackson, we need better options," Hancock said.

"What if there are no better options?"

"Then do what one of the previous administrations did."

"What?" asked Jackson.

"The twin towers."

"Isn't that just a conspiracy theory?"

"Conspiracy theory or not, it worked extremely well for the then-current administration."

"Thousands of people died."

"And everyone saw its impact." Hancock was trying to sell hard.

.   .   .

"You can't be serious," said Jackson, completely baffled.

Hancock looked him in the eye. Jackson felt a sudden urge to get away from this man, the man he had gotten elected as President. This was sick. But he said nothing in response because he didn't know what to say.

"Think about it, an attack on this country and people will forget about everything. This is what I need. You need to make it happen."

"I can't, and you shouldn't be wanting this." It took a lot out of Jackson to say these words. His confidence was wobbly. He thought he was staring at a mad man.

"This...this is the difference between you and an achiever, Jackson. So, either make it happen, or find another job. It's that simple." Hancock used his oft-used weapon. He knew a White House job was the greatest thing in this country and no one could comprehend losing it, even in one's dreams.

Jackson ran his hand through his hair. Hancock ignored it. Jackson then rubbed his face with his hands while taking long breaths. From the spaces between his fingers, he watched the laptop screen. His fingers then moved quickly on the keypad.

. . .

"My resignation will be in your inbox in a second." Jackson shifted his gaze away from the screen and spoke in the side microphone connected to the driver seat. "Stop the car," he said. The limo stopped to the side. Jackson opened his side door and with his bag in one hand and laptop in the other, got out. Hancock didn't expect this from Jackson, he considered a sleaze-ball devoid of morality, but he had just been proved wrong.

"Jackson, you are letting go of a golden opportunity," Hancock shouted from behind.

Jackson looked at Hancock one last time and shut the door without saying a word.

"Sir, should we move?" the driver asked though the microphone.

"Yes," Hancock snapped to no one in particular. He had a hard time believing what had just happened. He looked for the remote and switched on the limousine's television in a bid to distract himself.

# CHAPTER 11

HOUSTON

Olivia, twenty-one years old, had just begun work at the hotel. Onyx was a 7-star hotel at the Marina, an upscale shopping mall located in the heart of Uptown Houston. It was one of the landmarks of the city, with a retail complex, office towers complex, a private health club, and housed names like Neiman Marcus, Nordstrom, Saks Fifth Avenue, and Macy's. Olivia was happy that her first job was with a big brand like Onyx.

But it was turning out to be a rare weekend for Olivia. On one hand, she had to report to work for half a day to relieve a co-worker. On the other, Briella, her long-lost cousin from London, had imposed an impromptu visit on her. And with her she carried a huge shopping to-do list that Olivia would now have to navigate through.

· · ·

*As if London had a shortage of big brands.* Olivia thought.

"I'll be at the hotel till two in the afternoon, so you will be on your own," she warned Briella. Onyx was Olivia's first paying job, so she didn't want to do anything to jeopardize it.

"Not to worry, my cute cousin. I've already made some plans."

"What plans and with whom? You don't know anyone here."

"You stress a lot. Two of my friends are also staying at your hotel." Briella had met the two boys during her flight. Olivia was skeptical when Briella continued bragging about them nonstop, but on seeing the pictures her jaw literally dropped. Even in loose fitting clothes, she could make out that they both had great beach bodies. Their Instagram profiles were public, with followers in thousands. By the look of it, they both seemed legit.

Olivia finally decided that she didn't want to let half her off-day go to waste. She would join them once her shift was over, but first, she needed to feel ready. She took her clothes off and hopped in the shower. Half an hour later she came out, blow-dried her hair and decided to try a braid this time, making sure it wasn't out of control either. This simple meeting could turn out to be a date but she didn't want to go overboard with her look. She checked her wardrobe and took out her trusted baby pink short dress and high heels, a light jacket, a small bag, and beautiful earrings. She packed all this in a bag. Her plan was to change once her shift was over. Till then she would be in her hotel uniform. She applied a light makeup to accentuate her natural beauty. One hour later, she was ready for her job. Ten minutes after that, both of them were in a cab, heading to the Marina.

The decision to take the cab was Olivia's, since despite having six parking garages, the Marina's parking always seemed to be full whenever she needed parking the most. The car took some forty minutes to reach the destination. Olivia had been there a couple of times before but for Briella it was a different thing. Wide-eyed, she just soaked in the beauty of the place; it was so huge and lavish.

The boys were not ready yet, so Olivia decided to keep Briella company until they arrived. Some window-shopping later they were starving. The food court seemed the most logical spot, but Olivia was on a diet and the food court was not exactly for people like her. Everywhere she looked, there were burgers, deli sandwiches, French fries, and ice creams. Luckily, Briella spotted a 'Build-Your-Salad' counter, somewhat hidden from the main area, at the far corner of the giant food court.

*Perfect!* Olivia felt like jumping with joy.

· · ·

They stacked their salad plates with romaine lettuce, broc-
coli, sliced cucumbers, bell peppers, onions, and beets with
olive oil and lemon juice dressing. When they saw their
salads, it literally looked as though they had brought the
whole rainbow onto the plate.

They found a secluded corner, and by the time they
finished their food, Briella got a call. The boys were coming
to meet them. Once they arrived, Olivia took leave to start
her day at the hotel.

"See you soon," said, Briella, and hugged her.

"I will," Olivia chuckled.

━━━

Shahrukh muttered Allah's name under his breath. Sitting
in the passenger seat of a decrepit Ford Minivan, Shahrukh
could see the majestic structure of the Marina. Over the last
two months, it had been meticulously recced by a mole
planted in the city, and he and his team knew the layout like
the back of their hands. None of them felt that this was
their first visit to the place. All of them wore snug full-
sleeved t-shirts, Puma running shoes, a pair of dark
sunglasses and baseball caps.

The building started to expand in size as the minivan
rushed on the Hidalgo road before taking a sharp left turn

towards the McCue Road that led to the parking. The first
stop was where Shahrukh and Yakub disembarked the
vehicle right at the entrance to the mall. The minivan
dropped off the rest of passengers at three different points
and then made a U-turn, speeding away from the building.

Observing the Marina, for Shahrukh the first feeling was
one of shock. The place was filled to the brim with
hundreds of cars, people going in, people coming out. He
tried to imagine the place once they got into action, but he
got nothing. Training simulations were different. This was
reality. He looked at Yakub. He too seemed a bit taken
aback by the realness of it. No one was there to hold their
hands and show them the path. They were on their own.
All they now had was their training and their God.

⸺

Marina's security was overseen by a Pennsylvania-based
company known for its high-end security systems and a
flawless track record. As per the intel received thirty
minutes ago, forty-three guards were on call that morning
along with the facilities management staff and mall employees. Shahrukh knew that despite the tall claims of the
company website, most of these guards were recent high
school graduates and were barely above the age of eighteen.
Their training was measly, done to save time and money.

As planned, the team had already split into four pairs. They
were going to enter the building from four different points.
Shahrukh and Yakub walked towards the main entrance,

soaking its grandeur. At the gate, six guards using highly sophisticated security systems were vetting the visitors The boys carried nothing but their social security cards and a plain Casio watch. No money, no weapons, no nothing. The entry was a cakewalk. None of the guards looked at them after they crossed the entrance threshold. The boys knew the positions of the CCTV cameras and deliberately avoided looking at them. The baseball caps and sunglasses helped.

Once inside, they walked past the Nordstrom store on their left and then turned right towards Macy's. Passing several smaller stores like Chico's, Peloton, and Crazy8, they eventually came to the crossroads. Behind them was Tesla and Banana Republic; to their left was the West Alabama Street and in front of them was one of the two Onyx hotels – a 7-star property with more than four hundred fifty rooms.

This was it.

# CHAPTER 12

UNION SQUARE PARK — **MANHATTAN, NEW YORK**

Richard, a twenty-six-year-old sales executive with BMW, observed the silent protesters from his preferred spot at Union Square. He was neither a Democrat nor a Republican. In fact, he was one of those who were always politically incorrect when it came to anything, as per Lily.

Lily was the daughter of Ohio's Senator Rob Turner and that, according to Lily, automatically made her an authority on US politics. Richard chose not to contest this claim. For the moment, she was only his best friend and his childhood crush, but that was going to change soon, or so Richard hoped. He was planning to ask her out officially, and he expected her to say yes.

. . .

Right then he could see her standing among the protesters. She held a large placard, waving it in the air with all her energy. The cool breeze caressed her soft smooth hair, and she radiated an unique energy. She was meant to achieve great things and Richard wanted to be there for her, to be her support if she ever needed one. He looked at her with longing. One day, not far in the future, she would reciprocate his feeling for her, and he would be the happiest man alive.

He checked his cell phone. The New England Patriots were on the field. Richard didn't care much about the game. He only kept himself aware of it because of Lily. She was a big Brady fan. He raised his head and looked again at Lily who was busy talking to someone standing next to her. He saw her laughing, throwing her head back with elation, but it was the two young men standing beyond her that grasped Richard's attention. Wearing beanies, they were looking the odd ones out, even in this group of protesters. From their postures they didn't seem to be participating in the demonstration, but yet they were there. Fair, clean-shaven and in their twenties, they didn't appear to be shady but it was their eyes; there was something odd in the way they looked at the others.

Observing everything, as if waiting for something.

Richard looked in the opposite direction where he had seen a few law enforcement officers.

. . .

*Should I talk to them?* He thought to himself.

━━━

Khalid keenly observed the army of protesters flooding Manhattan's Union Square on the fourth straight day of rallies against President Hancock's policies. Police estimates had indicated that the number was somewhere north of a thousand. The day before, two people had been arrested, yet the crowd was in no mood to break down against the administration's crackdown. A group of people representing the protestors had met with the city's Chief of Police last evening. The police had agreed to allow the participants to continue the demonstration, but warned them not to stand on or climb the barricades placed in front of the park, otherwise they'd be arrested.

Homemade picket signs bobbed throughout the sea of protesters, several of which read 'HANCOCK — YOU ARE NOT A SUPERHERO' in bold black letters.

"We reject the President!" the crowd chanted as protesters started marching up Fifth Avenue. Some climbed the poles of scaffolding and stood on them, holding protest signs while pumping their fists in the air. Traffic delays and intermittent street closures were present throughout Manhattan in the afternoon, including the Union Square area and East 57th Street and Fifth Avenue.

. . .

Khalid had seen enough recce videos over the last two months to understand the ins and out of the place. It was a popular convergence point to hold rallies and protests due to its neighborhood — the Flatiron District, Chelsea, Greenwich Village, East Village, and Gramercy Park. The location was bounded by 14th Street on the south, Union Square West on the west, 17th Street on the north, and Union Square East to the east, linking together Broadway and Park Avenue South to Fourth Avenue. Also, many of the New School's buildings, as well as several dormitories of New York University, were at a touching distance from the square.

There was the impressive equestrian statue of U.S. President George Washington cast in bronze, along with the sculptures of Marquis de Lafayette, Abe Lincoln, and Mahatma Gandhi. There was also a Temperance fountain with the figure of Charity emptying her jug of water, aided by a child.

Standing at the center of all of this, Khalid soaked in the beauty surrounding him for the last time.

# CHAPTER 13

## FARMER'S TERMINAL MARKET — Philadelphia

It was an unusual morning in Philly. Unlike its usually wet and cloudy weather, today the air was nippy and the air dry and cold. Mary, a fifty-eight-year-old woman from Ambler, a tiny borough near Philly, found a quiet place to sit along the fringes of the main seating area at the Farmer's Terminal Market in the heart of Philly. Her son, Stan, accompanied her.

At the 12th and Arch Street in Center City Philadelphia, Farmer's Terminal Market was an enclosed public market, spread over two floors. It was a popular spot for tourists and locals alike, with over a hundred merchants on the ground floor. The entry was from Filbert Street in the South, Twelfth Street in the West, and Arch Street in the North. The seating arrangement was in a grid pattern with an open area at the center. The basement level had state-of-the-art refrigerated storage for the use of vendors. With more than 6 million visitors annually, the market remained busy year round.

Mary wore an easy smile and her eyes beamed with curiosity. She didn't have much going on, which was fine by her. Her gaze panned slowly across the expanse of tables, merchant stalls, and flow of customers ambling through the aisles. The market was a familiar place to her. She'd been coming here since she was young. These days she often came to the market alone or occasionally with her son, Stan, who worked in the Howard County Water Department. In reality, Stan was a part of the TF-77's best support team – Vesuvius. The job at Howard County Water Department was his cover. Mary was content that her son had a stable job with a solid 401K. After her husband succumbed to leukemia, Stan was all she had. Stan's job kept him busy but whenever he visited Ambler, both of them visited the market. He had no interest in the market, but he did it for his mother. The place was her constant companion when he was in the field, fighting the bad guys.

"I like sitting in a corner and looking at people. I like the movement; it tells me that I might be old, but I'm alive..." she had once told him when he asked her the reason for visiting the marketplace time and again.

"You're not old, mom," he had told her then, but she wasn't listening. He knew it wasn't just the people that drew her in. It was nostalgia. She used to come here with his maternal uncle, and his grandmother, strolling with them through the aisles together for hours, their arms gradually becoming weighed down with bags of groceries as they went. Nowadays, she often found someone familiar to chat with and sometimes even ventured to strike up conversations with complete strangers — especially when she sat at the bank of communal tables at the center of the market. She was happy to take the forty-minute train ride from Ambler to Philly several times a month, just for the feeling of being connected with her childhood, and establishing a connect for her son, Stan.

Today, like on other days, Mary was sitting at her usual place by herself while she waited for Stan, who had gone to the restroom. As she waited, she kept looking around, her bright eyes taking in everything.

Even at this time in the morning, seats in the central seating area were tough to come by. Many people, after scouting and hovering for a few minutes, wandered off to try to find one of the solo tables that lined several of the aisles, or simply find a small patch of space where they could linger long enough to wolf down a quick bite. Nearby, a middle-aged couple stepped away from the bar at Molly Malloy's and danced their way into the main seating area. A pair of late-teen girls wandered by, one asking, "How do you even decide where to go?" She saw a middle-aged couple rushing toward a four-person table that had just opened up and successfully grabbing it. And after they quickly settled in, a younger, twenty-something couple who were scanning the tables was invited by the middle-aged woman, who waved an arm and motioned to the two extra seats at their table.

"Are these free?" the younger woman asked, over the din of the other diners.

"As long as you don't mind sitting with strangers," the older woman said.

"Not at all!" came the reply. A moment later, the two couples began eating lunch together. Mary smiled.

Surveying everything, Mary thought of how there was always a certain vibrancy to the place that she loved.

*But for how long?*

# CHAPTER 14

FARMER'S TERMINAL MARKET — **PHILADELPHIA**

Saif, along with three of his men, walked briskly towards the basement of the Farmer's Terminal Market in Philadelphia, that had the state-of-the-art refrigerated storage for the use of vendors. Their familiarity with the whole place was uncanny. They knew what they were looking for and where they would find it.

*Storage 137.*

The thick steel door wasn't locked but no one could know for certain unless they pulled it with all their might, but no one did. Till last night, the storage space was under maintenance. A paper stuck on the door mentioned it clearly. But Saif knew otherwise. He grabbed the steel handle and pulled opened the door. Inside, under the shade of yellowish dimming light, they could see eight three-foot-long haversacks weighing at least thirty-five pounds, waiting for them. It was eerie how everything was right where they had been told to find them. Saif checked his watch. It was almost time. He stepped inside and opened the bag closer to him.

Inside the bag was a Kalashnikov assault rifle with a side-folding metal butt and ten 30-rounds magazines. Along with these, the bag had over five hundred rounds of 7.62 Soviet ammo rounds, fifteen to eighteen hand grenades, two SIG Sauer pistols along with six spare magazines and two 5-kg Improvised explosive devices (IED) with a programmable electronic timer switch programmed in their wristwatches. The bag also had a burner cell phone bought from the same city where they were going, a GPS handset with pre-fed coordinates on the maps and fake student identity cards from the local universities of the specific cities they were going to rip apart. Each of them picked two haversacks and slung them onto their shoulders.

They were now ready for war.

# CHAPTER 15

UNION SQUARE PARK, **MANHATTAN** — **NEW YORK**

Khalid Sheikh Mohammed and his buddy came out of the public restroom and moved briskly towards the basement of Union Square Park. In the restroom, they had left behind an IED, timed to explode an hour later. They walked among the thousands of protesters.

The other four pairs covered 14th Street on the south, Union Square West on the west side, 17th Street on the north, and Union Square East. As soon as they got into their positions, each of them zipped open their haversacks. Eight Kalashnikovs were out. They quickly slung their rucksacks on one shoulder, leaving their firing arm free, a shooting technique of the US Navy Seals, and opened fire.

# CHAPTER 16

ONYX HOTEL, **The Marina, Houston**

The guards at the door considered Shahrukh and Yakub guests of the hotel. Their confident walk and their seeming familiarity with the hotel made sure of that. They confidently crossed the fragrant, opulent lobby of the Onyx, and without looking at the giant chandelier hanging from the ceiling or asking anyone directions, glided into the lobby and turned left into a marble-lined corridor. At the end of it was a men's restroom.

Inside, a man was standing unusually close to the mirror, checking his face. As the two boys entered the restroom, he appeared slightly flustered and made a gesture of removing something from his face. None of them made eye contact. It wasn't a place to exchange pleasantries.

· · ·

Shahrukh and Yakub leisurely entered in the third and the sixth toilet cubicle. They took out the plastic cap of the in-wall flush toilet systems. Inside each, a small key was hanging with a thread. They didn't have to wait long to hear the restroom's door shutting with a click. The man had left.

First Shahrukh, and then Yakub got out of their cubicles and walked towards the only locker there. The two keys opened two boxes. Their eyes lit up. Inside, two haversacks were waiting for them. They took them out, unzipped them and took out the cell phones. They were charged and had only one saved number. After putting the cellphones in their pockets, they took out the Kalashnikovs, inserted the magazines and cocked their weapons. Opening the restroom's door, they walked towards the reception area.

# CHAPTER 17

CENTRUM, **a shopping mall in Phoenix**

The van had left Taha at the basement of the Centrum, a shopping mall in Phoenix, from where he was trafficked inside the mall by a covert ops team working for the Professor. An arrangement that was made in the other cities too.

Wearing a men's hooded, waterproof jacket generally used for hunting and fishing, Taha looked out of place in the mall full of people who were there to enjoy some family time. Observing his surroundings, he slowly crept up to the center of the first floor. People busy shopping, checking their cells and doing hundreds of other things ignored him and his out-of-place outfit because the face was as American as it could get. There wasn't any beard, or skullcap on his head, to raise any unwanted suspicion.

. . .

Taha looked around and then checked his Casio watch. The timer he had set thirty minutes ago still had four minutes. Two hundred forty seconds left to breathe before everything would be ashes and smoke.

Tiffany, a five-year-old girl, playing with her doll as she sat on a bench near the escalator, was watching Taha. Maybe the red color of his jacket attracted her or maybe his demeanor, whatever it was, her eyes were glued to him, watching what he was doing as he stood a few feet away from her. Her mother, sitting beside her, was looking in another direction at the time.

Taha observed the girl watching him, but he kept on with his ritual. He slowly unzipped his oversized jacket, took it off and dropped it to the floor, revealing a suicide vest packed with improvised explosives and armed with a detonator. To maximize the impact, it was further packed with ball bearings, nails, screws, bolts, and other objects as shrapnel. The small detonator was in his left hand.

Tiffany suddenly stood up. Her eyes were on the jacket that was now on the floor. It was the color of the jacket that interested her. With her tiny feet, she ran in the direction of Taha.

A man standing near the Nike showroom saw the toddler running and then his eyes moved towards Taha. His face suddenly drained of its color.

.   .   .

Almost at the same time, Tiffany's mother found that her daughter was not at the bench and instinctively looked around to find her. She soon found her. She watched Tiffany's short ponytail waving behind her as she ran, and then she saw where Tiffany was going, moving towards a man standing not far from where she was seated.

His left hand was raised in the air holding the detonator, and his eyes were fixed on Tiffany.

Tiffany's mother got up with a jerk; her shopping bags fell on the floor. She opened her mouth to scream but the horror of the moment froze the sound in her throat, and she watched helplessly as her child approached death.

Within a few seconds, almost everyone on the first floor froze. Watching Taha, they all knew what was going to happen. They could not run. They could not hide. They could only watch and pray to their Gods, wherever they were.

The four security guards at the entrance watched Taha from behind and slipped out of the door to save themselves. Little did they know that the IED was going to wipe out not only the building they were paid to guard but also everything in the five hundred yards radius around it.

.   .   .

Taha watched as the needle raced towards zero in his watch.

*Five seconds.*

He ignored everyone, only watching Tiffany, who, now closer to him, bent to pick up his red jacket. Getting up with the red jacket in her hand, she looked straight into Taha's eyes. A cackle escaped her lips. Taha involuntarily smiled. It was the effect of a child's laugh that he couldn't help himself but smile with Tiffany. A tear rolled down his left cheek.

*Two.*

Taha looked at the mother.

"No!" she screamed, finally.

*One.*

*BOOM.*

PART 2

# CHAPTER 18

MARYLAND, **United States**

Hundreds of questions spun in the air and Helms hoped that he would get some answers once Basit landed on American soil, but for the rest of them, he had to act now. He picked up his phone and dialed Samuel Baker's number. Baker was the White House Chief of Staff.

"Baker, I need to talk to the President. This is an emergency." Helms was right off the bat from the word go.

"Who's this?"

Helms didn't know how to respond to this. It took him a moment to realize that the man on the other side wasn't joking. Samuel Baker, the White House Chief of Staff, didn't have the number of the NSA director. The whole thing reeked of stupidity and scam.

*Are these the same people who are ruling this country?* he asked himself.

"This is William Helms — Director, NSA. Get me the President, right now." Helms somehow bottled his anger. He couldn't let his emotions take over his rationality.

"He is on his way for a game of golf with the President of North Korea. You'd have to wait for it to be over." Baker spoke calmly while sipping his coffee.

"I'm not sure if you've heard me, but this is an emergency."

"Every Tom, Dick, and Harry comes to the White House with this or that emergency. I cannot let the President get distracted by them."

"Listen, you piece of shit, either you get me the President right now or I will make sure that your career is over before this day ends," Helms thundered.

Baker took some time to respond, and then Helms heard him snigger. "The President has specifically asked me to keep morons like you away from him, so you can try, but I think it will be you who will be facing the axe," Baker hissed on the phone.

This was the first time in his life when Helms wanted to strangle someone with his bare hands. Baker wasn't just an idiot but also had a false sense of supremacy about his reach and power. But if what he was saying was true? If it was, then the President had taken the cold war against his own men, too far.

*What should he do?* Leaving things in the lurch and hoping them to take shape on their own wasn't an option here. He had always been a doer, and whether they knew it or not, the people of America needed more people like him for what was about to come.

The conversation with Baker had him worried. What if all of Washington was against him? He personally had no qualms about getting in the bad books of the White House or Capitol Hill but if it hampered his ability to get through the bureaucracy and reach the final decision-makers, then it was a problem, and a huge one at that.

He needed to check if he or the agency was being alienated from the decision-making. His next call was to the United States Secretary of Homeland Security, who didn't pick up the phone. His personal assistant did, who promised that she would make sure that her boss got back to Helms soon.

. . .

Helms then dialed Raborn, who disconnected his call. He tried again and was shunned again. It was frustrating. He felt he was confined in an invisible cage from where reaching out to anyone was impossible, but he had to try. There wasn't any other option.

His next call was to Patrick Mattis, the United States Secretary of Defense, who picked up his call on the third ring.

"Hello Bill, how are you?" Mattis sounded chirpy.

"We have a situation. My sources in Afghanistan have intel about a massive attack on the American soil today. The President is incommunicado. You need to take this to him and request an urgent meeting."

"Bill, hang on a second. I'm sure this is just another hoax. America today is not like the America of 2001. There is no 9/11 happening on our soil ever again. I heard you were on leave so just relax for a day. I'm heading out to my office. I'll see if I can reach out to the President. You know he is busy with the North Korean President."

"Hoax or not, we need to consider any such threat with absolute seriousness. And let me worry about my off-day. At the bare minimum, we should begin checking all pickup trucks, box vans, and semi-trucks headed into the major cities. We should also consider increasing security at the transport hubs and crowded places."

"Which cities are you talking about?"

"All the tier-1 cities, starting with New York, Washington..."

"Don't be stupid, Bill," Mattis interrupted him. "We don't have enough manpower and you know that. and also, we can't just shut our cities without any credible intel."

"This information is credible, and this is an emergency. You need to tell the President that this is happening today, whether he likes it or not. If you want me in DC, I can be there in an hour."

"Helms, I don't think that there is any need to spend taxpayers' money on unnecessary travel expenses. You should stay in Maryland, I'll see what I can do."

This was unusual. "Patrick, is there anything that I am not aware of?" Helms asked.

"Bill, it's not that."

.   .   .

"Patrick, we have known each other for twenty-five long years, and you know that I take bad news better than anyone else. If there is one, I'd expect you to tell me to my face."

"Bill, listen to me, do not come to DC and do not stay in your office. Go home and spend time with your family. I'll take care of everything."

"Patrick, it's not about me or my family, it was never about that and you know that. I called you to tell you that my intel is legit. It's your call now. If I don't get a call from the President in fifteen minutes, I'll need to find other ways to get this message out."

"Listen, Bill, don't do anything rash. I told you to take it easy. Let me talk to the man and I promise to get back to you as early as possible."

"Fifteen minutes, Patrick. That's all I can give you."

"Bill. I hear you, let me talk to the President. I'll call you back." Mattis didn't wait for Helms's response. It took Helms a few seconds to realize that Mattis had hung upon him. Was he really going to talk to the President? He decided it was better to deliver a summary report to Mattis just in case.

.  .  .

A moment later, Helms's office door opened. It was Andrew. "Sir, you need to see this." He switched on the television.

The newscaster was hysterical. "A minute ago, two near-simultaneous explosions have been reported at Phoenix and San Diego."

This was much worse than what Helms had estimated. The attacks had begun, and the world's most powerful nation wasn't the least bit prepared for them.

# CHAPTER 19

WASHINGTON DC, **USA**

The warning came in while the majority of Washington was in a weekend morning mood. The duty officer in the White House Situation Room received the call from the CIA Ops center. Within minutes, phone lines were buzzing around the capital and beyond. Calls went to Walter Raborn, the CIA director and the agency leadership. Simultaneously, security details were rousted, motorcades were sent out, and key players in the National Security were ordered to get to their respective offices immediately.

Patrick Mattis had just got off the call from Helms when the bad news reached him, and he was the first cabinet-level official who received it. Between his call with Helms and the bad news, he had three or four minutes which he spent thinking about what he would tell Hancock, or whether he should even tell him anything.

. . .

But now there wasn't any option.

---

Alone in the backseat, Hancock was deep in thought on what he should do next when he absent-mindedly read the scrolling tape at the bottom of the television screen. News about some hotel in some city. Which city he didn't know, didn't care, but then he started to pay attention.

Five blasts in three American cities, all within a span of minutes. A shopping mall and a luxury hotel in Phoenix, two malls in San Diego and a luxury hotel at Indianapolis were hit by what seemed at the moment like a suicide bomber attack. The names of the shopping malls and the hotels were on the screen.

Hancock was dumbfounded. He had only a vague concept of something like this happening to elevate his chances, but he hadn't properly considered the repercussions, if anything like that ever happened. It was a far-fetched idea unless someone took it upon themself to deliver it to him. And now someone had taken it upon oneself to deliver it to him, and he had no clue what he should do with it! The situation was unprecedented, and he was painfully out of his depth.

*The initial death toll is somewhere around 900 people with more than 2000 wounded,* the scroll at the bottom read. *The*

*9/11 attacks had a death toll of 2,996 people with more than 6,000 injured.* The nature of the blasts was not immediately clear and there were no immediate claims of responsibility.

As his motorcade kept moving towards the golf course, Hancock was still lost in thought when his phone rang. It was Walter Raborn, Director of the CIA. *He was the right person. He could help him.* Hancock picked up the phone before the third ring.

"Mr. President, have you...?" Raborn asked, stopping in mid-sentence.

"I know. Walt. " Hancock said nothing further. He knew it was an emergency but the question was, what he should do now.

"A team of the best CIA agents is already on the hunt to find out how it started," Raborn said, trying to steer himself clear of any political mess that these events would result in.

"Walt, join me in the Situation Room in thirty minutes. I have asked Baker to make some calls." Hancock lied about calling Baker, but he couldn't be seen as indecisive to his subordinates.

.  .  .

The Situation Room, officially known as the John F. Kennedy Conference Room, was a 5000 square-foot conference room and intelligence management center in the basement of the West Wing of the White House. Run by the National Security Council staff for the use of the President of the United States and his advisors, it was used to monitor and deal with crises at home and abroad. The room was equipped with secure, advanced communications equipment for the President to maintain command and control of U.S. forces around the world.

"Yes, sir," Raborn responded.

"Thank you, Walt." Hancock disconnected the call. He then spoke on the microphone to move the cavalcade to the White House. He needed to do something else too.

He opened his social media account and wrote: "I strongly condemn the cowardly attacks on our people today." And pressed the publish button.

# CHAPTER 20

UNION SQUARE PARK, **Manhattan — New York**

Khalid and his partner emerged out of the public restroom with heavy rucksacks on their shoulders. Richard's gaze had never left them from the moment they had emerged out in the open again. Their edgy body language and shifting gaze made Richard extremely uncomfortable. His eyebrows squinted with surprise. Something wasn't right and he could sense that. He hastily combed the crowd for Lily. She wasn't where his eyes had left her. He instinctively got up. He had to find her.

Khalid and his partner, unaware of Richard's movements, shifted the weight of the rucksack onto one shoulder while unzipping it. Their other hand reached inside the bag and emerged out holding an assault rifle.

. . .

Despite the distance, Richard instantly recognized the weapon. He knew what it meant, yet he couldn't believe that this was happening.

━━

The militants wasted no time opening fire. Shooting from the hip, targeting the crowd in precise controlled bursts while moving in opposite directions in a semi-circular arc. Their walk was confident and unhurried. Their targets were the thousands of hapless protesters and people who were in the park — men, women, and children.

The other three pairs were already in position. Their rucksacks open. Weapons out.

Seven of the city law enforcement officers were leisurely observing the gathering when they overheard the first burst of shots to their right. They instinctively turned and saw two twenty-something active shooters with assault rifles firing at the crowd. Seven 9mm semi-automatic SIG Sauer P226s instinctively popped from holsters.

What they didn't realize was that they were not dealing with just two shooters. Another pair of shooters, covering the Union Square West, were keenly eyeing the officers. As soon as they saw the seven men getting ready for some action, without second thoughts, two suppressed barrels turned towards the uniforms. The barrels breathed forty rounds in the next few seconds. The first twenty hit four out of the seven officers squarely on their chest, rib cage and face. Dead before they knew it. The three others took cover behind the nearest stationary vehicles. The barrels moved with them and the next twenty bullets pierced the steel sheath of the cars, but the officers were still safe. They quickly understood one thing, these kids were not just some amateur school shooters. They needed immediate backup.

One of the three officers took out his radio and yelled, "Multiple active shooters at Union Square Park. Heavy casualties. Shooters are armed with assault rifles, possibly AK-47s."

Another duo covering the North flank saw the three uniforms taking cover behind vehicles from the bullets coming down from the West. They both looked at each other and without exchanging a word, aimed their Kalashnikovs at their new targets. With their backs exposed, the three officers were sitting ducks for this duo. The guns blazed and the three officers' bloodied bodies hit the ground limply.

⸺

At the Union Square Park, the chaos was maddening. Men, women, the elderly and children ran in every direction for cover. It was screaming madness. The cries of fear, helplessness, and pain sounded as if someone was pouring molten lava into one's ears. But what the ones running away did not know was that they were running from one shooting pair only to get in the zone of the next shooter duo.

. . .

No one knew who the shooters were or why they were shooting mad.

Even before the first shot was fired, Richard's primal instincts had been to get to safety, but his love for Lily made him run to find her first. But he could not fight the rising wave of a maddened crowd. He got kicked in the gut and another kick crushed his knee. The blows were unexpected, and he hit the ground hard. As soon as he touched the ground, five people tumbled over him like falling pins. A barrage of bullets whooshed over. He didn't realize it at that time but the five people who fell on him were all dead. And with that they crushed every hope of his finding Lily. A few feet away from him, a pregnant woman squealed for help. Richard could see the blood on her maxi dress, but he was helplessly stuck. He looked at her with whatever degree he could manage to lift his head up. Their eyes met, and a bullet blasted through her skull.

The shooter's laugh ricocheted in the air. Richard suppressed his screams, digging his face into the dirt, hoping that he was invisible from the shooter's gaze. It was primal instinct at play. Self-preservation. Thinking about his family and Lily, his tears kept disappearing in dirt and blood.

*Nine minutes.*

Nine minutes later, the shooting paused.

Nine minutes later, the place was buzzing with the ghastly silence of the dead. The eight militants remained unconquered. The stillness was occasionally interrupted by weak cries for help from the survivors among the knots of bloody, mangled bodies and were instantly silenced by a bullet.

The shooters didn't care how many were dead or still breathing but one look at the massacre, and they knew they had made Yasin proud. The first leg of the mission was complete, and they needed to move on to the next. Khalid checked the time and tried to imagine the situation in other cities but then he jerked the thought out of his head. They had to stay alive to complete the next step of the mission and he had to make sure of that. He heard multiple police sirens screeching at a distance, cruisers racing towards the crime scene with urgency.

Khalid looked at the others and flicked his right hand. It was time to move. The nearby area had been deserted barring a few moving vehicles whose drivers didn't get the time to navigate to safety. The shooters fired at the few moving vehicles, but then they didn't want to waste much of their ammo on something that would not have the intended effect. Instead, they sprinted towards First Avenue. Their new target was the Bellevue Hospital Center, a mere one and a half miles away from Union Square. At the entrance, they saw a moving ambulance and shot three rounds. The driver wasn't prepared for an assault and lost control of the van. The vehicle rammed into the hospital's gates. The four unarmed security guards watched it unfolding and immediately sprang into action, shutting the hospital's doors, but Khalid foiled their plan with twenty rounds of lead.

Four more dead bodies at the gates. Though the hospital staff had already been alerted by the NYPD control room, they hadn't had much time to prepare themselves. Now the fight was at their door and they literally froze as the gunmen stormed into the hospital. One of the staff switched off the main light switch. Others started to lock down the wards to protect over fifteen hundred frightened patients.

# CHAPTER 21

FARMER'S TERMINAL MARKET, **PHILADELPHIA**

Mary was waiting for Stan when she heard the shots. Stan was still not back from the restroom. She saw people running in her direction. In a momentary confusion she looked around and saw that four men with guns were shooting with blinding rage at the crowd.

She got up from her chair as fast as her arthritis-weakened knees allowed her, her gaze fixed in the direction of the restrooms. But in the maddening rush of people, she could see no faces, only bodies rushing to get to safety.

She heard an approaching scream and located it a second too late. A man was rushing towards her. Behind him was a shooter who had just opened fire in the running man's direction. The bullets leaped towards the man's spine. Mary shifted her gaze back to the man's face and saw his expression freeze. His moving body jerked forward, and he lost his balance. Before Mary could understand anything, she was falling on her back along with the deadweight of that body. She hit the floor hard and a burning wave swelled through her spine. Her head hit the floor and bounced back. The concrete floor beneath her skull had started to get red. She fought hard against the blackness, but her weak body had already lost the battle. As she slowly slipped into darkness, all she could think of was Stan.

Lead rained through the market aisles from eight assault rifles from every exit point. The shooters moved forward, inch-by-inch, tightening the circle.

Stan was splashing water on his face when he heard the first couple of rounds and his first trained instinct was to duck. The sound was dreadful because he knew where it was coming from. His mom was out there waiting for him and his mind immediately wondered about her safety. His right hand went for his hidden leg-strap; his trusted SIG was there. He checked the magazines. Only one. Twenty rounds. No backup. That's all he had. He hadn't come here ready to face a full-blown terrorist attack.

He focused on the sounds outside and closed his eyes for a moment. Amidst the screams, he could hear something revealing. There was method in this madness. Focused short bursts. The consistent gap, between each fire. There were four distinct sounds frequencies. He couldn't determine how many shooters were outside, but the shots were coming from four directions. If he imagined it as a tight square, then the shooters were at the four corners of that square. He checked his phone to see any news about the shooting to help him ascertain the number of shooters. There was none.

He looked around and found the stall doors shut. People who were inside had probably heard the gunshots too and decided to stay where they were. Stan could do it too, stay in the safety of the restroom and wait for the massacre to stop but his instincts weren't going to allow him to go for that option. The biggest reason was the people outside, including his mom, facing bullets for no fault of their own.

In his crouched position he quickly covered the distance to the door. He pushed it open and immediately thanked the maintenance team for doing their jobs diligently. The door had made no sound. From the sliced vision, the first thing he noticed was the floor's color. As far as he could see, there was only red. He had no idea if any of the shooters were right outside the restroom. The shots were still raining down. Stan decided to get out. There was no point waiting for everything to be over. The attack was sudden, and he had doubts if anyone would have the firepower or the skills to stop the perpetrators.

The men's restroom's door faced the women's restroom and the passageway opened into a small foyer just as in the letter "T". The middle of the passage had space to get back into the market. Stan slowly crawled out of the men's restroom without opening the door fully.

Once he was out of the restroom, he saw a shop's steel counter. His truncated view showed the counter to be deserted. He trod cautiously forward and found an elderly man's lifeless eyes staring back at him. The man was possibly the owner of that counter. A gasp left Stan's mouth. He felt the pressure building up in his chest. These were the butterflies of mortal combat. He took a deep breath to control the adrenaline rush. It was necessary to get his focus on to the most vital task — of containing the attack.

He hoped to locate the shooters quickly, but before that, he had to find a solid cover. With no bulletproof vest to protect him, he knew that his success rate hovered in the negative territory. A SIG was no match for assault rifles. If the shooters got their eyes on him before he could spot them, the consequence would be definite death.

He carefully slithered forward in the foyer and slowly the passage started to reveal itself. From the corner of his eye, he also kept checking the women's restroom's door. He didn't want any surprises. Despite the chaos, the passage was untouched.

.  .  .

Soon another pair of lifeless eyes found him and then he met the third, the fourth, the fifth, and after a point, he had to stop counting. Amidst this, his gaze landed at a spot. A perfect cover. The only issue was that it was ten to fifteen yards away from where he was right then. The pathway to it was laid out in the open, but he had to take that risk. Bending forward he checked the passage one last time before taking the plunge. Luckily, there wasn't a single living soul lurking in the passage.

Cowering, Stan hurried towards the spot, his eyes darting from corner to corner to spot any danger. Fortunately, he found nothing.

Once behind the marked thick steel counter, he sat in a squat position among multiple dead bodies. The shooting had subsided but he could still hear an occasional burst of shots followed by shrieks of pain. He utilized the next few seconds to adjust to his new surroundings while scrutinizing them. The counter had an empty man-sized steel cabinet built to store unused containers, and it was unlocked.

He was still busy thinking of his next steps when two pairs of faint footsteps grabbed his attention. There was someone on the other side of the counter. Stan looked up and immediately found comfort in the height of the counter.

.  .  .

He sat still as one of the shooters thumped the counter with his hand, but the counter didn't budge. Its legs were latched onto the floor with some solid screws. Stan took the benefit of the thumping sounds to swiftly crawl inside the unlocked steel cabinet and close it.

Stan sat alert with his SIG ready to shoot anyone try opening the cabinet's door, but no one did. Maybe the shooter didn't know that counters had cabinets.

Sitting inside, he cocked his ears to identify the position of the shooters. Following the sound of the footsteps, he figured that no shooter was near the counter now. He slowly got out, his back against the steel wall of the counter, intently listening to the sound of footsteps. The shooters walked slowly, with the measured steps of predators looking for their prey. Stan moved with them on his side of the counter.

The edge of a gray rucksack emerged first, followed by the whole bag, hanging on a man's shoulder and partially open to easy access. The terrorist's back was towards Stan, but he wasn't alone. Another militant, scanning the other side, walked a couple of steps in front of him. They were the ones who had probably checked this side of the counter and had found no one.

The partially undone bag gave Stan the glimpse of the preparedness of these men. Discovering the arsenal engulfed him with a sense of unease but then something captured his imagination. *Hand grenades.*

There was a way, and he knew how it could be accomplished. He waited for the shooter to pause while he moved his gun from his right to his left. As soon as the man stopped, Stan carefully put his right hand inside the bag. His fingers wrapped around one of the grenades. Without drawing his hand out, he plucked the safety pin. He then left the active grenade in the bag and carefully drew his hand out. The shooter, unaware of this, walked further, following his partner in the lead. Stan retreated behind the counter. He had six seconds to get himself to safety.

One, Two.

He decided to get inside the cabinet, holding its door from the inside.

Three, Four.

The two terrorists walked closer to the next shooter duo lurking not far from them. They were busy checking every aisle on their side and happy that as far as they could see the aisles had only dead bodies.

.   .   .

Five. *Six.*

What Stan didn't know was that the haversack did not only have grenades. In a matter of seconds, the grenade blast combined with the RDX blew everything to pieces in its vicinity and almost made the high ceiling of the market, redundant. The building wasn't built to withstand such an intense blast, and neither were the bodies of the four militants. Rubble, shards, and shrapnel flew in every direction and caught the other terrorists off guard. Stan being closer to the attack felt the blow too despite being inside the steel cabinet. He had never expected the blast to be of this power and without the steel wall protecting him, he'd have suffered the same fate as of his enemies.

Inside the cabinet, he couldn't even imagine what had happened to the militants. A large portion of steel counter was blown away by the impact, but the rest of it remained grounded due to its nailed legs that held it together. The blast waves made Stan hit the steel wall with an intensity that almost made his left shoulder dislocate. The loosely held doors of the cabinet gave way and unbolted with a loud thud. The massive blast caused his ears to ring and his body shuddered involuntarily. Despite this, he didn't lose the grip of his SIG. It was the only thing that would keep him away from his death.

Outside the building, Police had already cordoned off the area with tens of Cruisers in position, but the unexpected explosion sent the whole setup into a tizzy. The concrete blocks flew out of the market with speed to wreck three Cruisers and badly injure five officers. Even the nearby Jefferson Station felt the tremors.

Stan's ears were still ringing. His left shoulder and rib cage had a stinging pain, but he needed to determine what was left of the shooters. He took a few seconds to realign himself and then carefully got out of the cabinet. Outside, the visibility had dropped to nil. There was dust and smoke all over. He couldn't see the roof but realized that since it was not on him yet, it probably was holding well. He rubbed his eyes to clear his vision, but nothing changed. The smell of burning flesh and wasted blood had started to overwhelm him.

The counter was ruined beyond imagination. Stan had survived because of the dual steel wall of the cabinet. If he had been outside, there was no chance he would have been in one piece to see this. Using the leftovers of the counter he slowly stood up, but in the effort his knees hurt like hell. He knew that he had stirred the hornet's nest, and more would come looking for the reason of the unexpected blast. In a way this was good since all he now had to do was wait.

And he didn't have to wait too long. A faint outline appeared in the dust, walking limply, with a rifle in his hand. The shadow stopped at some fifty yards away. Stan knew that the man might have spotted him too standing in the dust. But despite pausing, he didn't shoot. Maybe he was still considering if Stan was friendly.

. . .

*A costly delay.*

Stan brought his SIG to bear and immediately saw the reaction as the shooter's barrel came to life, sweeping across the area around him. But Stan fired first. The terrorist fired a millisecond later. They both missed.

Stan's bullet flew off-target, but it caused the shooter to flinch, which bought Stan half a second for a follow-up shot. He didn't miss this time. The man shuddered as the bullet punched his chest. But the hit couldn't silence the assault rifle. Glinting lead raced towards Stan and before he could duck and find a cover, one of the bullets tore into his belly. His shot-up adrenaline didn't make him feel anything. He squeezed the SIG's trigger again, firing the third round as fast as he could. It found the gunman's neck. His cervical column severed, the assault rifle was silenced. Stan knew that he had hit his mark.

Not knowing if anyone had lined up on his muzzle flashes, Stan decided to sit on his knees and immediately regretted that decision. "Damn it," he muttered. Somewhere in his abdomen region, blood had started to leak. He could feel that a bullet was inside.

Fortunately, no return fire came his way giving him precious time to slowly take cover behind the still intact part of the counter. While sitting, the immediate thought in his mind was to call Jessica – his colleague in the Vesuvius team. He lurched forward and took out his cell from his back pocket.

"Shit!" he muttered under his breath. It was broken.

# CHAPTER 22

FARMER'S TERMINAL MARKET, **Philadelphia**

Saif opened his eyes and watched the haze. Dust and smoke, with visibility hovering at zero. The blast had thrown him far away from where he was standing. The blast wasn't planned. Not even expected. He had no idea how it went off. The plan was to use the RDX to take down the whole building, but that wasn't until they had sprayed enough bullets.

Footsteps. Lots of them. The uniforms were coming in. His rifle was nowhere to be seen, and he didn't know where to find it. The untimely blast had ruined everything. They had failed in their mission. Now he had to find a way to kill himself.

. . .

With his right hand's support, he tried to get up, but his body wasn't ready. His left leg wasn't moving and hurt like hell. He lifted his head to see what was wrong with it, but the haze made it harder. The only way he could do it was by using his hands. His left hand started to scan his leg, and a cry escaped his mouth. Multiple steel rods had punctured through his left leg. The realization made the pain ferociously intense. Tears trickled down his cheeks. With both his hands, he swept around to find his weapon or something to kill himself, but all he could find was rubble and dust.

The boots were closing in. He looked sideways for his teammates to help him out. Nothing. He was alone.

━━━

Two tactical robots rolled inside the building, before the first man would put his first step in. Covering all bases, their job was to give the infantry a heads up on what to expect inside. The blast's impact was severe at the left flank of the market, but the rest of the building was intact, albeit in a mess. The steel counters had taken most of the impact on themselves, making sure that the age-old building didn't give way.

The two robots slowly scoped the area for any hostiles. The 360-degree cameras fitted at the top relayed the live feed to their operators' laptops. No hostiles spotted yet, but a large area still remained unswept. The SWAT team was doing everything by the book.

. . .

The first operator heard whispers and murmurs from the right flank of the market on his headphones, and the robot turned in that direction. Some thirty yards away, among the rubbles and dust, the operator soon discovered the first set of fearful eyes through the mounted camera. The flank had multiple survivors, still under a mild wreckage but breathing. The second robot, sweeping the left flank, found the first duo of the militants under the debris. Assault rifles in their lifeless hands. Their eyes open in shock.

"Two dead hostiles." The operator quickly informed his team through his microphone.

"Where?"

The operator gave the location.

"Anything on the right flank of the building?" The captain asked.

"No, sir."

"Update me once the sweep is done."

"Yes sir."

.   .   .

It took another thirty minutes before the sweep was completed. Then, slowly the SWAT team started to branch out in the market. The dust had started to settle, and the carnage had started to take a shape. The medics followed the officers, ready to tend the injured. The uniforms' first priority was to find the survivors.

One of the officers rushed to the two dead hostiles and squatted beside them to check their belongings for their identities.

"Medics needed here now," another officer yelled at the medical team.

"Sir, you need to see this," yet another officer hissed in his lip mic to the captain.

"What is it?" the captain asked.

"We have eyes on an injured shooter."

The captain didn't need another invite to spring into action. He was halfway through to the first hostile when his radio cackled again. Another terrorist spotted, and closer. He decided to change his destination while barking orders. Uniforms closer to the two terrorists moved in tandem to get in positions.

. . .

The first thing the sergeant closer to the second hostile saw was a gun similar to his own, a SIG, in the right hand resting on the floor. The man's back was partially visible, rested against a steel counter.

"Hands in the air where I can see them," the sergeant yelled. The man might be a terrorist, but he was on American soil and the law had to be upheld.

There was no response, as if the man didn't hear him.

"Hands in the air where I can see them," he yelled again. The man didn't even flinch.

"The hostile isn't responding. He could be dead," the sergeant informed the others behind him. The uniforms kept on tightening the semi-circle, their SIGs leveled at him.

The first sergeant loomed closer to the man and kicked his gun. It slid away from the man's reach. The second sergeant then slowly covered a big arc to see the face of the man from the right side. The man's eyes were open, staring into oblivion. His other hand was on his stomach. The first sergeant exchanged cues with the second and then inched forward. He held the hostile's hand to check his pulse.

. . .

"Need a medic here, fast," the second sergeant yelled. A minute later, one of the medics came rushing. The two uniforms took a step back to give him room. He checked Stan's vitals and then looked at the sergeants. His face explained everything. The first sergeant quickly checked Stan's pockets and found a wallet Credit cards, some papers, and a social security card.

The captain reached in time to hear what the medic had to say. "Cause of death?" he asked

"Possible excessive bleeding. Bullets in his abdomen region," the medic replied.

"Any id?"

"We have his SSN." His sergeant spoke this time. The man was American.

"Transfer the body to the morgue and find everything about him and his family. I'm going to check the second hostile," the captain ordered without battling an eyelid.

Two of the sergeants who had found Saif and his dead partner, amidst the rubble, stood in silence as a team of medics tried their best to get Saif out of the steel rods, alive. The blast had made one of the pillars fall on them, taking the duo by surprise. Two AK-47s lay a few feet away.

Occasionally the medics paused and checked the whole situation again. It was a delicate case; any haste would mean the imminent death of the man. Two others held Saif carefully while a third one cleaned the area around his legs to look more closely at the steel bars.

"I need him alive." The captain had finally reached the spot and fired his first order.

"We're trying our best, but you need to stop yelling," one of the two experienced medics snapped back at the captain. He knew his job and didn't need a reminder of what needed to be done.

"Let my boys know if you need any help." The captain remained unfazed by the rebuke and moved to check the rest.

Saif, who was semi-conscious, looked at the captain and his lips moved, whispering, "I have done what I came to do. Kill me now." The medics ignored his pleas. The two sergeants looked at each other and then looked at the captain who had just stopped in his tracks to listen to Saif's murmuring.

·  ·  ·

"I need him breathing. Make sure of that." He reiterated his orders to the two sergeants. They both nodded in the affirmative. He was a high-value capture, and they all knew his value.

# CHAPTER 23

ONYX HOTEL, **The Marina, Houston**

With their loaded Kalashnikovs held high in the air, Shahrukh and Yakub had stepped out of the men's restroom, into the reception area of the Onyx.

Once they were in range, Shahrukh started to fire blindly at the reception, killing eleven guests on the spot, and then flung a grenade that exploded near the reception counter at the far end. Yakub took care of the entrance, killing three guards. Two of the guards standing away from the entrance, seeing off some departing guests, heard the shots being fired and fled the scene before the bullets could reach them.

Both Shahrukh and Yakub deftly changed magazines and sprayed a few more rounds inside to ensure there were no survivors. The attack was brief and violent, lasting a little over two minutes. The shots, the screams, and the explosions were quickly swallowed up by the chaos of a busy Onyx afternoon. Once the shooting stopped, six more militants entered the hotel. They knew where they had to head next in the building and moved towards the first floor, where the rest of the haversacks were placed.

⸺

In the hotel, a couple was halfway through their meal at the Lobby Bar, when they first heard a firecracker-like sound, followed by the screams as people ran to take cover. They weren't alone. Three other tables were also occupied in the bar with guests having their breakfast. The couple saw a gun-wielding terrorist through the glass door of the restaurant and quickly ducked under their table. Shahrukh didn't enter the Lobby Bar but crossed it, looking for something else. Yakub walked behind him, firing from the hip into the elevator area, killing more guests. Shahrukh and Yakub's bullets crackled wildly down the shiny marble corridors. Then they heard the gunshots on the first floor. It could mean only one thing; the rest of the six teammates had found their rucksacks. Shahrukh and Yakub then rode an elevator to the first floor of the hotel, leaving thirty-something bodies on the ground floor.

⸺

Briella, along with everyone else present in the Marina mall, heard the gunshots and became immediately alert. The sound was coming from the Onyx, where Olivia worked.

· · ·

"We need to find her," she said, looking at one of the two boys she was with.

"It's not our job. Police will find her. We need to leave now," the boy retorted.

"But..."

"We are not heroes! It's a police job to save people. We can't do anything." The other boy tried to sound convincing.

"Everyone please, move towards the right-side exit." The announcement happened in tandem.

Briella still took out her cell phone. She needed to tell Olivia about the shootings.

———

Olivia mistook the shots fired on the ground floor for fire-crackers from the wedding reception organized at the Bellaire of the Onyx. She had just finished her second month as a trainee at the hotel and barely knew her way around the maze of rooms.

She was in the server room of the hotel on the second floor overlooking the poolside. The room was a converted guest bedroom. It was one of the most vital spaces in the hotel. Inside, floor-to-ceiling IBM servers streamed and backed up data from the Onyx's ninety-three hotels. The office was located directly beneath the grand dome of the hotel.

The shots continued. Then an explosion reverberated through the hotel.

Olivia immediately reached for her cell phone to call her mother, and saw Briella's missed calls. There was a message too: 'Shooting at Onyx. Hide'.

# CHAPTER 24

ONYX HOTEL, **The Marina, Houston**

Martha was in the kitchen when her phone rang. The ringer was on mute and she hadn't got the time to unmute it. The phone rang three times but no one picked it up.

Olivia searched desperately for her father's number. William Helms was in his office when he saw Olivia's name on his phone.

"Dad," Olivia was petrified.

"Olivia! What happened? You okay?" Helms immediately sensed the fear in his daughter's voice.

. . .

"Dad, I heard gunshots in the hotel. What's happening?"

"Gunshots?" *Was Onyx under attack?* Helms had no idea until now. "Olivia, stay where you are. Stay hidden. Don't go out. I will come and get you. Tell me where you are exactly?"

Olivia slowly explained the way to her office. Helms heard it with utmost silence.

"Dad, I don't want to die. Please, please come soon." She had started to cry.

Even someone like Helms, who dealt with life and death day in and  day out, couldn't control his emotions. His daughter was in danger and he would need all his strength and resources to save her and so many others who were in the hotel.

# CHAPTER 25

General David Shelton traveled to the White House with his four aides, one each from the Army, the Air Force, the Navy, and the Marines. The CIA director, Walter Raborn was also in the room. When the President and Raborn entered the Situation Room, the five military men simultaneously snapped to their feet. Raborn got up too. Hancock nodded in return and went to sit on his leather chair at the head of the table.

Patrick Mattis, the Secretary of Defense, Frank Allen, the President's National Security Advisor, and Samuel Baker, the President's Chief of Staff, arrived soon after, and were seated on both sides of the President. General Shelton glanced at Baker and then looked at the file. According to him, Baker was a nuisance, especially in a time-sensitive matter like this, and he didn't like his presence in the room, but it was not the time or the place to air his personal thoughts. It would have taken the focus away from the more pressing issues.

"Gentlemen, William Helms is with us via video conferencing," Mattis informed everyone.

Helms had just got off the phone from the FBI Director who was also connected via the video conferencing. He hoped that at the end of this, he would have some answers on how the offense would be planned, especially in Houston. On Mattis' insistence, he had not taken that flight to DC and now except the video-con, he had no way to be in the discussions. The agenda at hand was to apprise Hancock of his options and give him a realistic estimate of the time it would take to move the right assets into position. Full-blown attacks were underway for the last couple of hours and the snail-paced government bureaucracy still had no tactical plan in place to stop the mayhem.

"What's the status?" Hancock asked.

"Mr. President, three hours ago more than twenty trained terrorists attacked six American cities. A total of six cities have been hit. A mall and a hotel in Phoenix, two malls in San Diego and a luxury hotel in Indianapolis were hit by five suicide bombers. Union Square Park in Manhattan, Onyx hotel in Houston and Farmer's Terminal market in

Philadelphia were attacked by three teams of six to eight members in each. Of these three cities, Farmer's Terminal market in Philadelphia is now under control. Manhattan is the worst hit and the terrorists have taken refuge in a hospital near the Union Square Park. In Houston, gunshots have been heard from the Onyx, a 7-star hotel in the Marina mall," Mattis said.

"What about the casualties?"

"Exact numbers are yet to be determined but initial reports suggest that this is bigger than 9/11."

Everyone in the room let out an audible gasp. 9/11 was a black day in the history of America and a repeat attack of that magnitude had seemed unimaginable till this morning, yet now it was underway with no end in sight.

Hancock was seething with anger. It didn't matter that not long ago he was thinking about a similar attack to help his Presidency. But now he had no choice except to appear in charge and angry. Somewhere in his mind, he also hoped to find a scapegoat for this mess too. Because once the dust settled, the first question would be, 'How did this happen despite a glut of acronyms of the agencies working 24X7 to prevent just these kinds of attacks?'

.  .  .

A fuming Hancock asked, "An attack of this scale and no one had a clue?"

"Two special operatives from Task Force-77, during a mission in the Helmand Region in Afghanistan, had found out about this attack a few hours ago, and immediately relayed this information through the right channels. They have also captured a Taliban commander, who seems to be privy to this attack and can help us with more details. At the moment they are air-bound with the captive," Mattis tried to sound responsible.

Sitting in his place, General Shelton flinched with surprise. No one except Hancock noticed it.

"William Helms handles TF-77, right?" Hancock asked, his question addressed to no one in particular.

"Sir, TF-77 is the brainchild of both NSA and the US Army. So, William Helms and I both are the overseers of this unit," General Shelton responded.

"Did you know about this?" Hancock asked a pointed question to the General.

"No, not until now." General Shelton spoke the truth. Helms had not had the time to tell him about the raid and the aftermaths.

Hancock jeered, "Seems like you both have a lot to discuss then."

General Shelton said nothing but he was enraged about being put in the spot like this.

"What do we know about the attacks and what can we do to stop this immediately?" asked Hancock.

Mattis answered his question. "William has a theory on how this attack is going to shape up and what we need to do to stop it."

# CHAPTER 26

WILLIAM HELMS GAZED at President Hancock and the rest of them in the Situation Room via the TV screen, wondering how helpless the whole nation was right now. Despite his urgency, the attacks had already claimed hundreds of lives and the numbers were rising. And now his own daughter was also somewhere in the Onyx, struggling for her life.

As everyone in the room turned their eyes to the screen to look at him, he felt an unease engulfing his senses. On one hand, he wanted to drop in the information that he had tried to reach out to the President, but his efforts were thwarted on the President's own orders of keeping him at bay. But what would it help achieve in this situation? The condition demanded all hands on deck and rattling about an idiot seemed like an unwanted distraction no one would indulge.

.  .  .

Helms stared at the occupants of the Situation Room on the large screen in his office, looking at him with rapt attention, hoping he'd answer the question writ large on their faces — *What now?*

*What the hell now indeed?* thought Helms. However, he started to speak with grave seriousness. "On 26th November 2008, ten Pakistani terrorists in inflatable speedboats came ashore at two locations in Mumbai, India, where they split up and headed in two different directions. Over the next four days, these ten men carried out twelve coordinated shooting and bombing attacks across the city. More than 170 people died, including 9 attackers, and more than 300 were wounded. Only one assailant was captured."

He continued, "This attack was inspired by a similar attack that had happened on 4th March 1975, when eight Palestinian terrorists in two inflatable rubber crafts landed on a beach in Tel Aviv. They walked into the four-story Savoy Hotel that was a few yards away from the Jerusalem beach, the only building on that street that was brightly lit. They took ten hostages and were barricaded on the top floor with all the hostages. In the ensuing firefight, eight hostages lost their lives. Three Israeli soldiers, including their commanding officer, were killed. Seven of the terrorists blew themselves up, destroying the top floor of the building. Only one was captured alive."

"What do you want to say?" Hancock interrupted him impatiently.

.  .  .

"This is an attack on similar lines. The attackers are specialized killers, highly trained and fearless. All they know is to kill. We cannot negotiate with them. The only way is to contain them and kill them before they kill thousands."

"What about the hostages? What if they get killed in the raid?" Hancock asked. His hands were sweating. He didn't want to be the one who would give the order that could result in the killing of Americans on American soil. This would be a sure-shot way of kissing his political career goodbye.

Helms talked tough, "Mr. President, if we don't stop this madness right now then even your whole office won't be enough to count the bodies."

Suddenly the door of the Situation Room burst open, and Mattis' assistant entered the room with haste. He paused at the entrance for a second while his eyes darted from one corner of the room to the other. As soon as he found Mattis, he hastened towards him. Once near, he raised his right hand and showed Mattis what seemed like a note. Mattis glanced at it and his face froze.

He looked at the assistant and asked softly. "You sure of this?"

.  .  .

"One hundred percent."

"Okay. Keep me posted."

"Yes, sir." The man took an about-turn and with the same urgency exited the room, closing the door behind him.

Mattis waited for the door to be closed and then looked back at everyone. "We have just confirmed the IDs of the terrorists in the Philadelphia attack," he said.

"And?" Raborn asked.

"Americans. All of them."

# CHAPTER 27

Wick and Eddie sat in silence watching Basit's unconscious body, held by a seat belt, lolling both ways. They had to leave Josh Fletcher, the CIA agent Wick and Eddie were tasked to extract from the Taliban stronghold in Zangabad, at the military hospital. The doctors had refused to give him permission to travel. But for Basit it was different. They had orders to take him with them, and no doctor could stop them. After tending to him with basic First Aid, they had taken the next C-17, a military aircraft, for getting out of Afghanistan.

Getting in and out of a country like Afghanistan wasn't as simple as taking a flight from any city. To get out, US troops had to travel in a military aircraft to a nearby country and then take a chartered flight the rest of the way. The total flight duration was nearly fifteen to seventeen hours, depending on the weather and many other factors.

Wick and Eddie, after a journey of four and a half hours, had finally landed in Romania, from where a chartered flight was ready to take them to the USA. All this while, they had no access to the Internet, or any other communication modes. Although they hoped to get a chance to hook onto a network at Romania's airport, what they didn't know was that they would not be ushered inside the airport building but would be taken directly to their chartered plane.

The journey to Romania had been uneventful. Basit was unconscious and Wick and Eddie hoped that the interrogation team in America would be able to extract some more information from him once they get hold of him. But right now, all they wanted was some sort of network connectivity to get an update on the attack Basit had spoken about. What they didn't know was that as soon as they had hopped on to the aircraft, the first bomb had gone off.

During their flight of four and a half hours, America was drowned in unimaginable chaos.

They had hoped that when they landed in Romania, they would learn that everything was under control, as they had relayed everything to the best-positioned person in the bureaucracy echelon, Helms. They had no idea that the tables had been turned upside down for Helms.

At Romania's airport, they were escorted to the chartered flight that was ready to take off with its three passengers – Wick, Eddie, and Basit in a wheelchair. Wick and Eddie walked together while an airport attendant pushed the wheelchair. At the beginning of the aircraft's stairs, four security personnel stood at attention. Wick and Eddie watched them with curiosity.

"Your IDs, please." One of the four security personnel asked of them. Wick and Eddie each took out one of their many fake passports and extended it to the security. The man checked both their IDs keenly and once satisfied, he handed them back to Wick and Eddie. "Thank you, Mr. Alex, Mr. Charlie. Please transfer any weapons that you have into this bag. We will move them to the luggage section." He extended an open, small black bag towards them.

"Is this necessary?" Eddie asked.

"Mr. Charlie, this is only for your own safety."

"I only feel safe with my gun by my side."

. . .

"Sir, without this we cannot let you board this flight. Protocols are important as you yourself understand."

Eddie wanted to say something in return, but Wick placed his right hand on his shoulder. Eddie zipped his mouth. Wick took out two guns and slowly dropped then in the opened bag.

"Thank you, Mr. Alex. Magazines too."

Wick took out five magazines and dropped them in the bag without a word. The man moved the bag in front of Eddie who did the same, with a sour face.

The man looked at the unconscious Basit.

"Be my guest," Eddie hissed with sarcasm.

"We are good." The man said and moved aside, giving way for them to board the plane. The other security personnel followed suit.

Once inside, they looked back at the men through the window. One of them was instructing the only air stewardess of the plane about where to put the bag, and to hand it over to them as soon as they landed in America. Wick saw the stewardess nodding politely at the instructions. With butterflies in his stomach, he only came back to his seat once the door of the plane was shut and it started to move towards the runway.

The stewardess approached them with a short summary of the safety protocols. She was only going to serve three passengers, and it was better to tell them everything in person rather than doing the whole routine. At the end of it, she looked at Basit who was strapped to a seat belt, his head lolling.

Eddie's fierce stare silenced any question she may have wanted to ask regarding Basit, and she only asked them if they needed anything to eat or drink. Eddie answered her without looking at Wick. He knew Wick would have said *no* and Eddie couldn't stay hungry for the rest of the flight.

Wick, sitting in the next row, opened the Toughbook to check the news. While they were on the ground, he had hoped the Internet would work. So he had already plugged in the DoD designed mini device in the USB panel to connect to the Internet. As soon as the news websites started to open, the first thing that hit him was the body count. More than two thousand dead and the attacks were still continuing. He looked back at Eddie who was already gazing at him to ask if he needed anything to eat, but Wick's expression soon mirrored on his face.

· · ·

*What?* Eddie asked silently.

Something was wrong.

"Thank you," he said to the stewardess, while quickly getting up from his seat to walk towards Wick. Wick shifted his gaze back at the Toughbook and Eddie followed suit.

"What the hell!" Eddie exclaimed as soon as he scanned the headlines.

Wick responded with silence. His eyes were busy scanning the news report for more details, trying to figure out the modus operandi of the terrorists. Eddie sat beside him as the stewardess came back again to ask them to buckle their seat belts, blissfully unaware what was going on in the other part of the planet. Wick and Eddie absent-mindedly buckled their seat belts while slowly digesting each bit of the news report.

They then checked their emails. There were none. No one in TF-77 except Helms knew that Wick and Eddie were on their way to the USA since their return was not planned for months. Helms himself had arranged all the logistics with some help from Wick's handler, Riley. Wick decided to send a message to Riley whom he knew was obsessed with checking her email every second minute and was very prompt in her response. So, before the connection might get lost, he needed to drop her a one-liner email, which he did. "Need details of attacks; esp. Houston and Manhattan. Need a support team on standby in both cities." Then he hit the send button. The page loaded for a few seconds before it showed the notification that the email was gone.

The plane had left the taxiway and was ready to take off. The two pilots were checking the systems one last time when they got an emergency message. *Effective immediately, all the USA airports are closed for any incoming or outgoing flights due to ongoing terror attacks.*

The pilots did not have time to think about the why or the how. They had received the notification from the ATC and even though it was not for them specifically, there was no point in flying to a country where they could not land.

The captain looked at the first officer and said, "We need to inform our guests that they might have to spend some more time in Romania."

"Let me give this news to them personally," the first officer offered.

The captain nodded. "I will start turning the plane back to the hangar."

.   .   .

Wick had already started trying to figure out the strategy behind these attacks. 'Why these cities and why these locations?' He closed his eyes and imagined himself in the place of the terrorists. If he had to plan an attack like this, what would he do and why? By the looks of it, the militants had come ready for shoot and scoot. But something was amiss. Something wasn't making sense. He jerked his head back and forth, rubbed his forehead to get it out, but nothing.

The first officer was addressing them now, "Gentlemen, we have just received an information bulletin. All the airports in the USA are closed for any takeoff or landing, until further notice. We have to get back to the hangar and unfortunately you'll have to wait in Romania till the coast is clear."

Subconsciously, hearing the first officer speak, something clicked within Wick. The team in Houston would have to be the most prepared one. Once they got in, they would wait till the coast was clear. Using the hostages, they might get a section of media on their side. He had seen this happening in a hostage situation like this. The rest of them might come with the intention of 'destroy and move' but this team in the Onyx had to come with the intention to stay put. The longer this standoff continued, the more the terrorists would gain. Wick's thoughts solidified with each passing second.

"We will head to Houston," he spoke loudly.

.  .  .

The first officer was surprised. Wasn't he clear earlier? "Sir, we cannot land in the USA."

Wick looked absentmindedly at the first officer. The stewardess stood behind him. Wick's hand moved fast and unbuckled his seat belt. In a fluid motion, he rose from his seat and took a step forward. His right hand swiftly slid inside Basit's coat and when it reappeared, a Berretta was shining in the reflective lighting.

He pointed the barrel at the first officer, looking into his eyes. He asked, "Can a single pilot fly this plane?"

"Sir!" The first officer had suddenly started to sweat. A shriek escaped from the stewardess. Eddie looked at her and raised his finger to his lips to signal silence.

"Can one pilot fly this thing?" Wick repeated his question.

"Yes...sir."

"That means we don't need one of you." He cocked the gun.

"S...sir!" The first officer stuttered.

. . .

"Eddie, tell the captain that you will be his first officer and we are taking off for Houston now. If he says no, then you know what you have to do."

Eddie walked towards the cockpit.

Wick tilted his head and looked at the stewardess who stood there, stunned into silence. "Ma'am, you should sit down and strap yourself in. We are about to take off."

"You too, if you don't want to die." Wick signaled the first officer to follow suit, and he complied too.

After a hiatus of ten excruciatingly long minutes, the plane started to move, and it meant that Eddie had done his job. But Wick had to tell someone in his team that they were heading for Houston. He grabbed his Toughbook and started typing, while keeping an eye on his two new hostages. "We are heading for Houston from Romania. Help us land safely. Need a support team outside the airport. Send the team's details. Need weapons. Only precautionary measures. Inform Helms." He plugged in the chartered flight's details and pressed send. He could now only sit and hope that the attacks would probably be contained, at the least, by the time they would land.

# CHAPTER 28

BELLEVUE HOSPITAL CENTER, Manhattan

Forty-year-old Doctor Reid Adams was at the end of a life-saving surgery when the OT's lights went off. He looked at Kevin and Brian, the two doctors assisting him and Martha and Patricia, the two nurses in the OT, and they seemed confused too. No one had any idea of what was happening on the first floor of the hospital. Reid signaled Martha to go out and check if it was just the OT or the whole floor.

Martha nodded and walked towards the door. She pushed the door open. Outside, the hallway was dark and deserted.

*'It's only afternoon,'* she thought to herself.

. . .

"Security!" she yelled, and immediately she heard footsteps in the direction, where she knew there were stairs. She closed the door behind her and impulsively turned towards the faint sound. A couple of seconds later, a man appeared at the far end of the hallway, at the edge of the stairs. In the dark, it took her a moment to realize that the man was neither a patient nor one of her colleagues. Something that looked like a gun hung from his right shoulder, its barrel pointing at the floor. The man too saw the silhouette of a petite woman standing in the hallway, unsure. Without warning, he leveled the barrel at her.

Dr. Reid had decided to follow Martha out to investigate the reason for the lights out, and he was just about to open the door when his hand froze at the doorknob. Successive gunshots in the hallway had shattered the silence. He looked at the other three, Patricia, Kevin, and Brian, and found his own fear reflected in their eyes.

"What the hell is going on?" Patricia asked no one in particular. Her tone was hushed.

"I don't know, but we're getting out of here. Move it! Kevin, lock the main door. We're taking the back stairs." Dr. Reid had involuntarily taken the responsibility of getting the four of them to safety. The three of them followed Dr. Reid to the back door of the operation theater, reserved only for the medical staff.

.   .   .

Every hospital had rooms, doors, and stairs, only available to the staff. The visitors or the patients had no idea about these. There were no signages either to help them identify these 'officials only' pathways. Dr. Reid hoped that whoever was shooting in the hallway was one of the lunatics high on TV shows and loneliness and would leave them alone if he found the rooms locked.

"This isn't going to work...we better use the elevator," Kevin said.

"Shh." Dr. Reid put his right finger on his lips. "What the hell is that sound?" They all stopped in their tracks and listened hard. And then they saw it, a cat. They heaved a collective sigh of relief.

Kevin heard Brian faltering on his feet. "Brian, you okay?" he asked. Brian was getting breathless and almost collapsed on the floor, his head in his hands. No one knew what it was, could be a mild panic attack, but they had no time to find out either.

"Calm down, you're going to be alright." Dr. Reid spoke carefully, making sure to keep his voice down.

In the parallel corridor, they heard footsteps clanking on the floor and they looked at each other with fear. Brian heard them too. He was already trying hard to soothe his nerves, but his fear had returned with extreme ferocity.

"We'll be fine. Now, let's hurry." Dr. Reid encouraged Brian, when a door not far from them opened and a hand grenade rolled over in their corridor.

*Run!*

Dr. Reid helped Brian get up. Kevin clutched Patricia's arm and started to run in the opposite direction. He opened the first door he found unlocked and pushed Patricia inside. Reid and Brian entered behind her followed by Kevin who then quickly shut the door behind him. The grenade blast rocked the corridor behind, but quick thinking and the steel door had saved them by a whisker.

It was a general ward and the four of them stood in silence in the darkness. No one moved. The fear of getting caught was very real. As their eyes got accustomed to this new dark, they lay on their bellies and started to crawl underneath the beds. If they made no sound, they possibly would be able to get out of this nightmare, alive.

Lying on the floor, Kevin checked on the others while looking in every direction he could possibly check while keeping his head down. And then a face appeared out of nowhere in front of him. A familiar face. Mr. Quinn, a man in his seventies and suffering from dementia, was on the floor like Kevin.

Quinn's eyes rested on Kevin, maybe he was trying to recognize him, but Kevin knew that he wouldn't be able to even if he wanted. His brain cells had already stopped giving a shit about faces a long time ago. Quinn, like Kevin, had no idea why the gunshots, but he knew that it wasn't good. So maybe he himself thought of cowering under his own bed or maybe someone from the hospital staff had helped him. Whatever it was, Quinn was at least hidden. The only problem, his bed was the one nearest to the main door.

Kevin signaled Quinn to crawl towards him with both hands, just to make him get away from the door, but Quinn got further confused. The only way to get to Quinn, was to crawl up to him and drag him to safety.

Kevin was mulling his options when the door near Quinn's bed opened. A set of boots, boots that did not belong to the hospital staff, approached the first bed, the very bed under which Quinn was hiding. Kevin knew that the boots were not friendly, but Quinn had no idea, and he crawled towards them.

Quinn sobbed, "Doctor help me! I don't know why I'm on the floor. Do you know where my wife is?"

.   .   .

The man in the boots stopped at the cry and squatted beside Quinn. A pistol appeared in his right hand. With his left, he grabbed Quinn's collar and without any warning put a bullet in his head. Quinn couldn't even understand what had happened to him. His brains wasted on the floor.

Kevin turned his face to the other side. Reid and Brian did the same too. But it was Patricia who was finding it impossible to believe what had happened. An innocent patient was shot without any reason and none of them could do anything. She almost shrieked but couldn't, as if her fear had grabbed her throat. Her tears flowed uninhibited, but she kept quiet.

The man grabbed Quinn's leg and dragged him to the door; then left him there to keep the door open. The militant then walked away, probably to find other targets. Once they felt that the killer was gone, Reid whispered from behind, "Let's move." He himself crawled away. Brian followed him but a hand gripped his right leg. He looked back. Another patient who had been in a road accident.

"Help me! I don't want to die...!" the patient cried.

Brian tried to turn back to help him and jerked his leg to smooth his movement. The patient's grip loosened, letting his leg go free. Their eyes met.

·  ·  ·

The other door of the ward opened, and someone entered the room. The visitor looked at the yelping patient and shot him twice at the back. Brian saw his eyes going lifeless. The man then grabbed his foot and dragged him away. Brian's fear made him crawl further under the safety of the bed, taking as little space as was humanly possible.

As soon as the killer took the dead patient out of the ward, the four of them crawled out into the other side of the ward where a door was semi-open.

Patricia was the first to enter the darkened corridor that had a large window where it ended. Sunlight lit up the corridor, and she suddenly saw an opportunity to escape. Getting up as fast as she could, she ran towards the window, shouting for help.

"Here! Over here!"

Khalid heard Patricia's cries on the other side of the hallway and walked fast to turn at the corner. He immediately saw an easy target. He aimed his pistol at Patricia's back and shot three rounds. She was almost at the window. The momentum of the gunshots further pushed her moving body into the windowpane. The bullets penetrated her body and emerged out leaving big holes, smashing the window glass. Patricia's lifeless body jerked forward. Dr.

Reid who was behind her at the exit hid in time behind a stationary table kept near the door. His eyes widened as he saw Patricia's limp body hitting the windowsill and then disappearing. Moments later he heard a thudding sound.

He forcefully muffled his screams. He heard the shooter's footsteps approaching the table, and he didn't know if retracing his steps back inside the ward would be a good idea.

Khalid stopped at the table, his eyes staring at the windowsill, where a moment ago there had been a human being. Dr. Reid made himself as small as possible. Any movement meant death. He did not dare look at the killer but he still couldn't stop the smell of death from surrounding him.

Despite the darkness, Khalid could've easily found his next target cowering near his feet, if only he had looked down, but his eyes remained focused on the window. He could hear the police chatter outside the window, and he couldn't give away his position. He turned around and went back to the safety of the darkness. He still had a lot of things to accomplish.

Kevin and Brian who were still in the general ward behind Reid were shell-shocked at the turn of events. In a matter of minutes, their world had turned upside down. Two of their colleagues were dead.

. . .

Kevin checked Reid who seemed to be frozen in place. He seemed to have no strength to tread further. Kevin knew that their safety lay in movement. He walked forward in his crouching position in order to pull Reid back into the ward. As soon as he reached Reid, he checked the corridor and from behind the table, saw one of the militants shooting at someone else. He looked back at Brian and Reid, and with his right hand pointed at the next opened door. Brian moved first and quickly covered the distance in the same bent position.

"Doc, let's go," Kevin whispered, shaking Dr. Reid. Reid looked at Kevin as if he had woken up from a long slumber. "We need to move," Kevin whispered while pointing at the door. Reid's eyes moved to where Kevin was pointing, and he saw Brian's back. He followed him without question. Kevin followed the two and as soon as he was inside, Brian locked the door. Reid, who was now back in control, blocked the door with a heavy steel table.

The sound of the table in the deserted corridor attracted the attention of the shooters.

Inside, the three of them heard footsteps approaching and saw the door trembling. The door was locked from inside and the thumping on the door grew exponentially high within minutes. The door looked like it could give up any minute now.

Outside the door, Khalid ordered two of his men, "You two, go and cover the adjacent corridor."

Inside, the three of them were panicking.

"What now?" Brian asked.

"This way. Come on." Reid signaled towards the room's second door.

Kevin pushed opened the door but then had to slam it shut immediately.

The two shooters had torched the corridor. The fire spread quickly and without warning, spreading onto the stairs. That corridor contained mostly general wards. All locked. The fire in that corridor meant that whoever was inside would soon be dead because of the heat and the suffocation.

"It's ugly down there. Check the other door!" Kevin shouted. Reid opened another door that led to the adjacent corridor but found the way blocked by patients and a few nurses. All scared but unhurt till now.

.  .  .

"What's going on?" one of the patients asked Reid.

"Everything will be alright," one of the nurses tried to console him.

"You need to run. Don't stand out in the open. Hide now." Reid yelled at the group. Hearing the warning, the group suddenly started to scramble in all directions. Kevin and Brian pushed through the crowd.

Suddenly, the militants appeared at the far side of the hallway and started shooting with a vengeance. But the three of them managed to drag as many people as they could with them inside the two opposite wards nearby.

"Get down!" Brian shouted. Kevin sprinted towards the door. Reid was in the opposite ward. Once inside he turned back to close the door and saw the nurse who was consoling the patient, lying inert in a pool of blood in the corridor.

"They are here." They heard one of the shooters shouting and rushing towards the wards. Reid's eyes met Kevin's who was standing at the edge of his ward and they both shut their respective ward doors with full force. Others jammed the door with beds and cabinets.

.  .  .

"Stay away from the door. Take cover," Kevin shouted. Reid was doing the same in the opposite ward.

The militants banged the doors. Soon more joined them.

"Wait." Khalid suddenly seemed alert.

Kevin and Dr. Reid heard the commotion silenced, but the shooters were still outside, they knew.

Militant #1: "What...?"

Khalid: "Someone is coming."

Militant #2: "I cannot hear anything."

Khalid: "Shut up and listen."

Meanwhile, Kevin looked at Brian, "We're sitting ducks here. We need to leave this room." The only way out was the ward's large windows. 'Could they jump and still be alive?' Kevin wondered. But he didn't know. On the ward on the other side, Dr. Reid was thinking the same thing. 'There were patients and there were nurses. Would they survive the jump from this height to the ground?'

. . .

There was no more banging on the doors.

Dr. Reid and Kevin listened hard.

*The silence outside was eerie. Had they left?*

CHAPTER 29

DESPITE KILLING AS THEY WILLED, Khalid felt an uneasiness. It seemed as if the noose was tightening on him. The hospital was now a deserted playground. The rooms were either locked or vacant. Wasting bullets on the people inside wasn't prudent. The approaching footsteps and the darkness made him question his training and belief system.

"What should we do?" one of the shooters asked. Khalid remained silent. The uniforms were inching closer.

"What now?" The shooter shook him wildly. Khalid looked at him with disbelief. He was back to *his* reality. He was fighting for his brothers and sisters. He had to avenge them.

"This is it. This is our moment of truth. We'll fight them. This floor is now our fort. We will kill or die." Khalid's voice was feverish. Others raised their guns in unison. This was their training's last lesson. Kill or die trying. No other option.

They quickly took positions: two each at the two staircases, and two each at the two windows, using the sidewall as their cover.

Waiting for the uniforms, Khalid checked his watch and a derisive smile seemed to appear on his lips. Over the next ten minutes, twelve vehicles were going to explode on the streets of Manhattan, Houston, and Philadelphia. Three each at the Farmer's Terminal Market and at the Union Square Park and six in the parking lots of Marina and Onyx.

# CHAPTER 30

ONYX HOTEL, **The Marina, Houston**

On the second floor, Olivia locked her office, switched the lights off and ducked under the table. She pulled the intercom along with her. The wired set was connected to every other telephone in the hotel. As long as it worked, she would find someone to come and save her. The office had glass partitions separating it from the rest of the space. A few minutes later, she saw the silhouette of a man in the hall, busy checking every cabin, opening and closing the glass doors. A rifle hung from his right shoulder. She retreated further under the table, furiously praying, sweating and crying incessantly.

The shooter was two doors away from Olivia's office, when something captured his attention. It was the sound of soft music coming from the adjacent corridor. The militant moved away.

. . .

Olivia heaved a sigh of relief, semi-collapsing on the floor when she heard a gun-blazing and a blast, followed by screams. Then she heard a loud bang at the west wing of the hotel. It had multiple guest rooms. She could only imagine what was going on in that part of the hotel.

The grenade blast had started a fire on the second floor. Fueled by the powerful centralized air conditioning system, the choking smoke had started to spread across the second floor. In the darkness, Olivia couldn't see it, but her chest started to burn. Her lungs badly needed fresh air but going out of the room wasn't going to save her. The whole second floor had turned toxic.

The heat finally switched on the water sprinkler on the second floor.

# CHAPTER 31

ONYX HOTEL, **The Marina, Houston**

Mike Noyon was lying on the carpeted floor of the
Monarch Room of the Onyx towers, looking at the
hundreds of bodies lying on the floor, limbs tangled with
each other in the darkness. Bullets raged through the room
in quick succession above them.

Mike and his wife were here to attend the wedding of their
dear friend's son. The place held a special place in their
hearts. This was the same venue where they had their own
daughter's wedding a few months ago. The gentle music
and the hubbub of the guests were occasionally broken up
by the sounds of what people perceived as the clamor of
some construction going on in the hotel.

. . .

No one paid any heed when two young boys appeared outside the glass door. They both smiled looking at the care-free guests, enjoying the wine and soft music. Then, two guns were leveled against the glass door and they pressed the trigger. The glass door shattered with a loud noise. The first few bullets pierced through a couple dancing near the door, throwing their lifeless bodies onto the carpeted floor. The two militants didn't stop there. Moving further into the room, they shot at anything that moved. The room echoed with the sounds of smashed cutlery, broken glass, flying wood, and the screams of hundreds of guests. A few people at the far end of the corner took out their cell phones. They needed to let someone know about their situation.

"Hello everyone," one of the militants spoke loudly to the still breathing people in the room. "So, how is everyone doing today?"

# CHAPTER 32

## ONYX HOTEL, The Marina, Houston

Eight officers from the Houston Police Department (HPD) were near the Marina when they received the call on their radio. They were told of gunshots at the Onyx in Marina. When they reached the hotel, the gunshots had silenced but they could see the dead bodies outside the hotel. After much deliberation, the team decided to enter the building through the entrance at Sage Road from the loading dock 'L'.

Without knowing the building's blueprint, it was impossible to navigate through the corridors. The hotel's security manager eventually stepped in to help them navigate the hotel. But that was not the only problem. Initial reports had indicated the presence of two young shooters and the team had planned the infiltration keeping this number in mind. Armed with the semi-automatic SIG Sauer P226 DAO service weapons, the team's aim was to take control of the hotel, but what they didn't know was that these were not just some street thugs or gang members.

They realized this truth as soon as they reached the hotel's reception lobby.

Shahrukh had known what would happen, and he had placed two of the boys in search of any moving target from that direction. So when the officers arrived, a barrage of fire came their way. The officers fired in return, but the semi-automatic guns weren't enough to counter the two heavily-loaded Kalashnikovs. Eight against two and still the stakes were heavily skewed in favor of the two militants. The fire was strong and there was no way these ill-equipped officers would be able to overcome it. The best thing was to with-draw the attack for the time being.

The retreat was swift and sudden. The eight officers made sure they provided sustained cover fire before the terrorists could gauge and understand their strategy.

What they didn't know was that this failed attack had suddenly given the terrorist an impetus to fast track their plan.

# CHAPTER 33

ONYX HOTEL, **The Marina, Houston**

Barring the two gunmen manning the first floor, the rest of them had started to comb each floor for hostages. Their instructions were clear – *Capture as many hostages as possible, kill those who fail to comply.*

Shahrukh had chosen Onyx's tenth floor's ballroom as their operations base for the next few hours.

Tactically, they were fortifying their position while the various agencies scrambled outside to prepare for a response to this massacre. Over a hundred Houston police department officers, many of them armed with the latest weapons, and tens of Cruisers, converged at the Marina but none of them entered the premises.

· · ·

They were waiting for the Marines or the SWAT teams to act, but the eight terrorists were not going to wait. They knew what they had to do. Three of the militants landed at the top two floors of the hotel with bottles of liquor from the Lobby Bar. Kicking open every suite, they drenched the walls, floors, drapes, and carpets with alcohol and set them alight. This was because Shahrukh knew that the Americans would try to enter the hotel and the most effective way to prevent them was from the top. The burning top floors would not only diminish that possibility, but the erupting flames would also strongly announce to the world that only a handful of people could bring the most powerful nation to its knees.

The whole of America saw the red flames flaring up at the top of the building. This and the twelve simultaneous blasts sent the TV and Internet into a tizzy. Every channel was ablaze with live images of destruction in every city. Every reporter with a mic and a camera started to propagate every plausible theory with extreme confidence without discerning how it would affect their audience's psyche. Several news reports started to flood the Internet that the White House itself was under attack. In the blind race of getting the biggest 'breaking news', these media avenues broke every journalism rule ever written.

The fog of war had enveloped everyone. Extreme panic had set across cities. From all across the country, false alarms were reported from multiple establishments, crowded locations and every place that anyone ever thought could be bombed. Panic-stricken citizens started to call 911 about anyone and everyone they suspected to be a terrorist in their vicinity. No one – neither the people nor the administration – knew what was real and what wasn't. In a matter of hours, it started to seem as if thousands of terrorists had taken over the whole of America.

The siege of America had begun: an audacious operation planned with military precision and ruthlessly executed in the heart of the USA.

# CHAPTER 34

YASIN WAS WATCHING everything on the TV screen, clapping and shouting. At the Taliban mission control rooms especially set up near the Durand Line (Afghan-Pakistan Border) and at the secluded location in Texas, twenty Taliban handlers, were also at work. They were wearing headsets and speaking English, Urdu, and Punjabi into the Internet telephone connections on eight laptops to motivate and direct the eight shooters at the Onyx. The rest of the shooters didn't have mobile phones, but for Onyx, Yasin had other plans. Each one of the eight shooters were provided with burner cells with only incoming call facility.

The control rooms had TV sets tuned to various American news channels and every social media channel, where Americans flocked regularly, to monitor the narrative and if required, then steer it in the direction they wanted. The other aspect was to get the latest updates and know how the American forces were being mobilized.

•  •  •

The information communication revolution had transformed the world. It was now, in an unprecedented way, helping the transborder terrorist masterminds exercise military-style command and control for the duration of the attack.

PART 3

# CHAPTER 35

OVAL OFFICE, **WHITEHOUSE, 5** HOURS SINCE THE ATTACK

President Hancock was pacing back and forth in the Oval Office. Samuel Baker, his Chief of Staff, was the only one accompanying him, and at the moment Baker was gazing at his boss with anticipation. Even after ninety minutes of intense discussions in the Situation room, Hancock wasn't sure what steps to take next.

The information that the terrorists were Americans and not from the usual suspect countries had made the situation trickier. He had already asked the FBI Director to start interrogating the families of the identified terrorists as discreetly as possible. He knew that sooner or later this would come out in the media and his decision and actions would be scrutinized from all angles. He was on a slippery slope, and with him was his legacy.

. . .

That's why he needed someone like a Peter Jackson at such crunch moments. Peter was an expert in getting the best out of even the worst situations and this was one of those. But Peter had quit a few hours ago. Hancock didn't want to call him to reconsider his decision. That would make him look weak. The US President could never look weak. Peter could be the Einstein of political maneuvers, but it was Hancock who was the President of the United States, based on his own merits and hard work. And he would bend for no one. If Peter wanted to go, then he didn't deserve to be in the White House, and that was that.

Baker, unaware of the contradicting thoughts going through the mind of his boss, was in his own world. For now, he was just glad that Helms had not revealed their conversation on the phone, but he had to talk to him and if necessary, apologize, to douse the impending fire. But he didn't want to do it in person. Why would he waste his time to travel to Maryland? Even if he had to cede his ground, he would do it on his own terms. The best way was to do it on the phone, quick and easy but not now.

# CHAPTER 36

HELMS KNEW he wasn't going to be a part of the Situation Room meeting anymore. After listening to his thoughts, Hancock asked him to log out of the meeting in the politest way possible. Helms was just disappointed that Hancock's personal agenda trumped national security in his case.

The downside of this was that he had no idea what was happening in the Situation Room, what decisions were being taken, and that made him jittery. On the other hand, he was constantly getting bombarded with intel on the terrorists' movement in the three cities. He knew that the same intel was also routed to the Situation Room, but he couldn't fathom why there was a delay in arriving at critical decisions. The more Hancock waited, the worse the attacks were getting. The number of lives they could have saved were reducing fast due to the Government's lack of action. Philadelphia was under control but what about Manhattan and Houston? Especially Houston, since it was now turning into a massive hostage situation.

·   ·   ·

Finally, he called Mattis. As soon as the call was picked up, he asked, "What's happening?"

"The President has taken a ten-minute recess."

"Recess!" Helms couldn't hold back his surprise.

"He needs to think this through. There are Americans involved on both sides."

"Yeah, but one side is killing the other so whether American or not, we should act now. We act when a lone shooter goes berserk on a school. How is that shooter any less American than these terrorists?"

"This is different, Bill. You are not getting it."

"Then explain to me, Patrick. I want to know what I am not getting, and you all are." Helms' bottled anger was now visible through his words.

"I've to call you back. The President is here." Mattis disconnected the call, leaving Helms again in the dark.

# CHAPTER 37

OVAL OFFICE, **WHITEHOUSE**

"What's the latest situation?" The first question from Hancock was in the air as soon as he entered the room.

"Philadelphia is under control. The SWAT team has taken over the market. Six terrorists are dead, and one has been captured alive. He is severely injured and unconscious. A team of doctors is working hard to resuscitate him. The reports are that a man named Stan Lang helped contain the attacks but unfortunately, we couldn't save him," Mattis responded.

"I need everything on him, and keep me posted on that terrorist's situation. We just cannot afford to lose him," Hancock ordered. "What about the other cities?"

· · ·

"Manhattan and Houston are now turning into a hostage situation. In Manhattan, the terrorists have taken over a hospital and an estimated fifteen hundred plus hospital staff and patients are in the building."

"Which hospital?"

"Bellevue Hospital Center."

Hancock's face displayed shock on hearing the name. It was the same hospital where his children were born.

"A SWAT team is stationed outside the hospital ready to engage and waiting for orders."

"How many men?" Hancock asked.

"From our side, twenty men against seven to eight terrorists. More reinforcements are on their way to the hospital."

"What about Houston?"

"Houston is worse. The terrorists have taken over the Onyx building. More than four hundred guests and hotel staff are expected to be in the building. A team of eight local police officers initially tried to enter the premises but the terrorists thwarted their efforts. They have also started a fire on the hotel's top two floors and the rooftop. We are trying to douse the fire using helicopters, but the birds cannot go near the building for the fear of getting shot at. We are awaiting orders from you on the next steps."

Hancock heard all this silently and then spoke, "General Shelton, what can we do?"

General David Shelton looked at his four aides, one each from the Army, the Air Force, the Navy, and the Marines. He then spoke with caution. "Sir, we should not make any decision in haste."

General Shelton knew what he was talking about. The Mogadishu incident had forced the American forces to refine their strategies. In Mogadishu, Somalia, in 1993, nineteen Army Rangers and Delta Force operators were killed in a daytime raid that had spun disastrously out of control. The conclusion to this failure was: never operate during daylight if you don't have to, and if you're not sure what you're up against, don't go in without close air support, or armor, or both. In this case, they had no idea what they were up against, so General Shelton didn't want to add another layer of complexity by conducting the raid in broad daylight. They had to wait for the night. But there was only one problem. Hancock wasn't onboard with this plan.

Worried about the negative press and a resurgent opposition, he had to look decisive, and not only in the Situation Room but also outside.

"General Shelton, we cannot wait till night. We have to act now."

"I'm asking you to wait while we try to gather intel about the terrorist. We are also awaiting reports from the Philadelphia attack so that we'll have more clarity. If we go now, we expect heavy casualties from our side too. It can also backfire if the terrorists start using hostages as a shield."

"General, we are constantly hearing gunshots from the buildings so our people are already in danger, dying. Don't you think the more we delay the more we are giving these terrorists a free hand? We have to proceed with the mission now."

General Shelton looked at others but none of them came forward in his support. After a long pause of deliberation, he shook his head in negation. Despite the President's insistence, he could not endanger the lives of the hostages and his men.

"General, are you saying you won't do it?"

.  .  .

"Not before we get more relevant intel."

"General, you know what this means for your career?"

"I understand, sir."

Hancock looked desperately at others, but none of them appeared inclined to interrupt to take anyone's side. They knew that a four-star general was no pushover.

Hancock had to take action now to show his strength. As the President, he could've overridden General Shelton, but that scenario had more downside than up.

However, he could obviously mobilize the local police teams, and he did that without waiting. He looked back at General Shelton one last time and started instructing everyone else in the room.

Hancock looked straight at others who didn't dare deny him what he wanted. "Let the SWAT team know that they are authorized to proceed as they see fit. Start with Philadelphia. If the operation is successful, then we will replicate it in Houston. Can we see the operation on the screen here?"

.  .  .

"Yes, Mr. President," Mattis responded.

"Do it."

Yes, sir."

"Try engaging the terrorists in the Onyx using dialogue. What's the status of their families?"

"Some of them have been already contacted. Multiple teams are now en-route to the various cities to meet the rest. The identification of the rest of the terrorists is still a work in progress."

"Did we get any updates on the terrorists hiding in Onyx and Bellevue?"

"Not yet."

"Keep at it."

"We are, sir."

.  .  .

"What about the press? Have we issued any statement yet?"

"No, sir." Baker responded this time.

"Work with Sandra and show me a statement for the press in thirty minutes."

"Yes, sir." Baker nodded and rushed out of the room.

# CHAPTER 38

JESSICA WAS in her one-room apartment in Todd Mission watching the deadly attack unfolding on the television when a number flashed on the cell that she used when not in active duty for Task Force 77. Being a part of the Team Vesuvius, one of TF-77's support teams, she was accustomed to leading a dual life. This call was nothing out of ordinary.

Vesuvius' job was to support TF-77's assets in their missions. These teams were typically comprised of three to four members — made available to field operatives depending on the mission's complexity.

Jessica led Vesuvius. She was the logistics liaison and an expert in close combat. Stan and Mac completed the team's trifecta. Stan was a former Marine and an Olympic-level shooter. Mac was the 'go-to guy' for anything remotely associated with technology. Together these three represented one of TF-77's ace support teams.

"Am I talking to Ms. Jessica?" The receptionist on the other side spoke in a soft tone.

"Yes, who's this?"

"I'm calling from the Hahnemann University Hospital. Do you know anyone with the name of Stan Lang?"

"He's my colleague. What happened?"

The receptionist looked at the officer standing at the other side of the reception desk. He nudged her to go on with the conversation.

"Ma'am, we found your name on his list of emergency contacts."

"Is he alright?"

"I have Sergeant Root with me to answer your questions." The receptionist looked at the officer and handed him the phone.

.   .   .

"Hello Ma'am. Sergeant Root here."

"Sergeant, what's the matter, is Stan alright?"

"I request you to sit down."

Jessica's heart sank. She knew the drill as she had done it multiple times in her previous role before joining TF-77.

"I'm fine, tell me." She articulated every word with great focus.

"Ma'am, during the terrorist attacks on the Farmer's Market Terminal, our team found Mr. Stan in the building. I'm sorry to say that when we reached him, he had already succumbed to injuries. The medics couldn't do anything to save him."

"Cause of death?" Jessica tried to control the pitch of her tone.

"Possibly, excessive bleeding...but an autopsy report is still awaited."

.   .   .

"What about his mother, Mary?"

"She is injured, still unconscious, but out of danger. The doctors are taking care of her."

"How did this happen?" The questions kept pouring out of her.

"We are yet to ascertain the cause, but initial reports suggest that your colleague was the one who helped to stop the gruesome attack at the market. We have found that the bullets that matched his gun were the cause of the death of one of the terrorists. Also, the blasts that killed four other terrorists were nearer to his location. Our best people are still working on adding the pieces together." Root took a pause to gauge the situation at Jessica's side. "Ma'am, are you okay?"

"Yeah." Jessica took some time to respond.

"We might need you here in Philadelphia for a few formalities once the flights resume operations."

"Yeah, I'll be there."

. . .

"Thank you, I'll be in touch. I have already sent you my number so call me if you need any help." Root took a short pause, then said, "I'm sorry for your loss."


Jessica disconnected the line without a response. Her emotions had taken a toll on her speaking capacity. She had spoken to Stan just the night before and she could still hear his laugh. And now she didn't know what to do. Should she call the TF-77 command center to let them know about the tragedy and take care of the proceedings? Should she call and tell Mac? What should she do?

# CHAPTER 39

Martha Helms switched on the news and found that Onyx was on fire. The first thing that came to her mind was — Olivia! She quickly grabbed her cell, lying face down on the dinner table and found multiple missed calls from her daughter. She called back. The phone on the other side rang too but wasn't picked up. She thought of calling her again but then saw the headline on the television screen: *Onyx still under siege.* The reporters had no idea how many people were inside and if they were dead or hiding or captured. What if Olivia was in the building and captured? The thought itself made her giddy with fear. Millions of unanswered questions invaded her mind. Only one person could have the answers, her husband.

▭

William Helms answered the phone after three rings. Banished from the security briefing in the Situation Room, he was trying to overcome this shun while sitting alone in his office. As soon as he saw Martha's name on his phone, Olivia's face appeared in front of him.

Olivia was their adopted daughter, and both Martha and he were proud of her achievements and how she was leading her life. Now she was trapped in the burning Onyx. An envelope of guilt engulfed his vision, and he blamed himself for not being there for her when she needed him the most.

Martha's voice invaded his thoughts. "Bill, where is Olivia?" Martha was on the verge of tears.

"Martha, don't panic."

"Where is she?"

"Onyx." He told her the truth and heard her dropping to the floor.

"Martha...Martha...you okay?"

"Bill...I want her back. Get her home. Please, I beg of you."
Martha had lost the grip on her phone but picked it up
again with tears in her eyes as she begged her husband.


"I will, Martha, I will," Helms promised her, even though
he didn't know if he would be able to keep this promise.

# CHAPTER 40

**ONYX HOTEL, The Marina, Houston**

Olivia waited in the darkness without making a noise. The realization that her father couldn't come to her rescue at a moment's notice had finally dawned upon her. Now, till the rescue teams arrive, she had to remain invisible, but an office surrounded with large glass windows was not the best place.

She could hear the guns cracking in the adjacent lobby and the sound slowly grew louder. While she was contemplating what to do next, a few stray bullets flew around the server room, shattering the glass, making her retreat further in.

She watched a shooter duo move past the office doors. And then they instinctively decided to go up to the pool-facing rooms onto the next floor. The bullets in the other part of the hotel had not ceased to rain. Grenade blasts reverberated like mini earthquakes through the atrium.

She had no option other than to wait. As the shooters vanished from the floor, Olivia decided to take refuge in the room designated for the Onyx employees. She checked her pockets and found the duplicate keys to that room.

With racing heart, she crawled out from the safety of the table under which she was hiding and squatting, moved towards the door. She turned the doorknob anticlockwise, incessantly praying that her God must at least give her enough time to get to the hiding place safely.

Outside, the lobby was deserted. Emergency lights were switched on, giving the lobby a haunted feel. With her back towards the wall, she moved away from the stairs and deeper in the hallway. On her way, her eyes wandered to the blood splatters on the half-shattered glass door of the Monarch – an Onyx ballroom. From her place she could see multiple dead bodies inside the Monarch. Gasping with fear, she instinctively zoomed forward. She could do nothing for the dead.

As soon as she saw the door of the employee room at the end of the hallway a smile of relief appeared on her lips, but it didn't last long when she heard faint footsteps coming in her direction from the opposite end of the hall. She paused for a moment, confused, wondering whether she should go and unlock the door, or retreat. The footsteps were getting closer. Unlocking the door now would mean that she wouldn't have enough time to get in the room without getting spotted. She checked the door nearest to her and found it locked. It had to be. The hotel security system only allowed the people with the hotel key cards. There was no time to check her luck with the other doors. '*Monarch*', Olivia's desperation was palpable, '*I could hide there.*' She took off her pencil heels, held them in her hands and started to run in the opposite direction. The floor carpet subdued the noise.

As soon as the Monarch's door appeared in sight, she accelerated. The footsteps behind her quickened too, inching closer. She just didn't have time to open the door and in a moment of panic, she jumped inside the room from the semi-broken glass door and landed on the broken glass pieces. A shriek almost escaped her mouth. Her feet and palms started to bleed as the shards of glass cut her soft skin. With no time to feel her pain, she got up on her feet and inched towards the farthest corner. The footsteps, as if following her, had arrived too close for comfort.

But she couldn't run anymore; her legs refused to support her body. The glass pieces had slowly carved themselves inside her flesh. In her haste and the darkness, she hobbled over one dead body and then another. Finally, losing her balance, she fell on the floor. This time she couldn't stop her cries. Her face hit the floor and her nose started to bleed. She instinctively covered her face with her right hand and the glass pieces stuck in her palm slashed her face.

Her cries magnified but she couldn't do anything. Someone was at the door, peering inside the room. She could not see who it was, but she dared not move. Lying still and closing her eyes, she prayed for her life.

# CHAPTER 41

## BELLEVUE HOSPITAL CENTER, Manhattan

Captain Luke McCarthy had waited long enough. He hadn't received the orders he needed. Inside the hospital, the terrorists were doing whatever they wanted to without any opposition. The delay in decision-making was costing lives every minute and his city was drowning in deep despair. Except for the SWAT team and the local police force, none of the other forces were there. It was baffling. Luke checked his watch and then looked at the phone. There was no call. And then a glass broke somewhere. He checked around for the source of it but found nothing. Suddenly someone grabbed his hand from behind and pulled him back. He wasn't ready for it and he fumbled on his feet trying to regain balance.

"What the..." he wanted to say a lot of things to the one who had done this to him but then the glass shards hit the ground where seconds ago Luke was standing. He looked up and involuntarily took a step back. A woman had jumped out of the broken window, freely falling to her death. Her body hit the ground and was smashed to pulp. The people around gasped. Some of them covered their mouths in shock. There wasn't any chance to save her.

Luke looked back at the window for anyone lurking there and checking the body. There wasn't anyone. He then looked back at the dead body and his bottled rage found a vent. In that moment, he decided to take the matter into his own hands. He was about to give orders to his boys when his phone rang.

"Luke, we have the orders to engage. Kill those bastards."

"Yes, Sir," Luke said with earnestness. He disconnected the call and looked at his team. "Boys, we are going in. Take positions." He then spoke on his lip mike. "Snipers, be ready."

He was not in a mood for mercy. These men didn't deserve it. His law told him that any such attack was punishable by death and he and his men would give them that.

———

Khalid stood in silence as the footsteps approached the third floor where he and his men were holed up.

. . .

"We're about to get hit." One of his teammates alerted him.

"I know," Khalid spoke without looking at his man.

"What now?"

"I don't know."

"We should hold them off and see if we can negotiate something using the hostages. We just need one or two people." The man didn't even believe his own words. That what he had just said would even work. Negotiate with whom? And for what...safety? What safety?

"They are not here to negotiate with us. They are here to tell us lies until their sniper gets a clear headshot," Khalid said it as a matter of fact.

"So, what now?"

"Slam RDX on each door. We fight and if we start losing, then start exploding the floor. Kill as many as we can before we get one ourselves. Whatever it takes to avenge our brothers."

. . .

"Whatever it takes." The seven of them repeated after Khalid.

# CHAPTER 42

## BELLEVUE HOSPITAL CENTER, MANHATTAN

Six men in body armor were already on the second floor, checking each ward. Two of them covered the lift and four covered the stairs. More joined them soon. Snipers were stationed at the adjacent buildings.

Khalid and his men were on high ground here and had better chances in this battle. He and his men had fortified all possible entry points on the third floor.

"Let them come," Khalid spoke to everyone in a hushed voice. His whispered message reached to everyone, and they all nodded from their positions. They sat still in the darkness.

·  ·  ·

A man's head popped up to check the third floor. It looked unusually silent. He threw two smoke bombs on the floor and then reverted to his cover position. Khalid and others watched the projectile fly into the hallway and reached for their masks.

A second passed. Two seconds. Three. Four. And then they heard the footsteps on the stairs. Five men appeared on the stairs in quick succession amidst the smoke. Khalid and his men let them arrive unimpeded. He wanted them to be in full sight. As soon as the last man appeared on the floor, Khalid's men opened fire.

The gunshots made the floorboards vibrate. One uniform hit the ground instantly. Others scrambled to find a place to hide on the third floor.

Khalid stopped firing but his men didn't. Using the cover fire, he took out a grenade and rolled it in the direction of the men. The four uniforms saw the grenade slowly rolling and stopping five feet away from them. If they ran, the rain of bullets would catch them and if they did not, they were already dead. They decided to take their chances.

Without second thoughts, they got out of their hiding location and ran towards the stairs. Khalid had already trained his gun at their exit and his bullets caught one of the four cops on the back. He stumbled on the floor and hit the deck hard. Dying instantly.

.  .  .

Another cop had gotten just halfway before he was shot. Now he was crawling towards the stairs when the grenade went off. The other two lunged over the railing and landed on the stairs below. Khalid gestured to two of his men to run to the floor above.

———

In the Situation Room, Hancock and everyone else watched the intense battle on a big screen. The skills of the terrorists had taken everyone by surprise. Three of their men were dead within the first thirty seconds of the battle, without even making a dent.

———

"Incoming through the exit stairs. Prepare to return fire," a terrorist yelled.

"Affirmative," someone responded in the darkness.

The uniforms took up positions behind heavy armored ballistic shields. A man popped up and raised a tear gas gun. Khalid and others watched the projectile fly in the hallway. It hit the floor and rolled forward. Another man popped up and fired another canister, and then a third. The hallway began to fill with smoke.

.  .  .

"Fire when ready," Luke said as he led his men from the front.

He watched his men as they opened the door entirely and began taking their positions, while deflecting any incoming fire from the terrorists with their heavy, armored, portable ballistic shields, designed to provide protection from 7.62mm AK-47 rounds. The weapons used by Khalid and his men.

Luke's men kept checking the area through a small window near the top of the shields while securing defensive positions.

"Let's go," Khalid yelled, and the gunfire started. The maelstrom was so strong that Luke's men couldn't even get up to shoot back from their ballistic shields. But Luke knew this would stop eventually when the guns ran out of bullets and they would have to stop for a reload. He proved to be right very soon. Despite the huge ammo at their side, Khalid had miscalculated how much he and his men could afford to use in one go. And as soon as they stopped, Luke's men rose from behind the shields.

"Now!" Luke yelled.

His men aimed their guns and started to shoot. Khalid and the others ducked for safety, but the locked wards and rooms gave them little cover. And unlike them, Luke and his men were tactically better in finding the targets and then pressing the trigger.

The two terrorists on the fourth floor walked towards the exit stairs from where they had planned to ambush the uniforms from behind. As soon as they opened the exit door, they met three gun-barrels pointing at them.

"Going somewhere?" The three men didn't wait for them to answer before squeezing the triggers. The two terrorists did not even get the chance to lift their guns.

At the floor below, it was a massacre on both sides. The terrorists had reloaded their weapons and were now back in the battle. It was now or never for them.

"Allahu Akbar," Khalid yelled as he blew the head off of one of the cops. Luke saw his key men going down and his rage doubled.

But for Khalid the situation was much worse. His plan to ambush the team from behind had not materialized. It wasn't even ten minutes in the battle and the end was almost near. His men were dying left, right and center.

.  .  .

"We should surrender," Omar yelled amidst the firing. "We are the only ones left." He was right. It was only Khalid and Omar in the battle now.

———

In the Situation Room, the mood was changing. Watching what was happening in the dark corridors of the hospital, Hancock and the others had started to feel that the battle was already in their favor. It would be a big victory for Hancock, going against the experienced General. He was already thinking of how he would be able to free Houston soon after this and maybe in two hours he could be boasting about his acumen in front of the international media. General Shelton would be the scapegoat. It was after all he who had suggested delaying the operation to the night.

———

Khalid wanted to tell Omar that they would keep fighting, but by the time he could say anything, Omar's body was already riddled with bullets.

Khalid was now the only one against an army.

Soon, Luke realized the absence of opposing fire and ordered his men to stop.

"I'm ready to surrender," Khalid yelled from his place.

.  .  .

"Throw down your weapon," Luke shouted, in no mood to take chances.

Khalid threw his gun and the haversack in the hallway.

"Come out slowly. Hands in the air."

"I'm American. Don't shoot me," Khalid yelled.

"Come out slowly. Your hands in the air," Luke repeated.

"I'm coming out."

Luke and his remaining men waited patiently for the shooter to appear in the open. Everyone in the Situation Room waited too.

Khalid appeared in the hallway, his hands in the air. Multiple flashlights on him had almost blinded him. His eyes were closed. He was completely at the mercy of his enemies.

"I'm American. Do not shoot. I surrender," he yelled again.

.   .   .

"On your knees. Now!" Luke yelled.

Khalid followed orders. "I'm American." He repeated the phrase again.

"On the floor. Now."

Khalid followed orders like an obedient student.

Luke and one other officer moved forward, keeping their shields in front, their guns trained on Khalid. Luke signaled the other officer to handcuff Khalid. The officer moved as per orders and immediately saw the detonator in Khalid's hand.

"Shit."

Lying on his back, Khalid smiled and pressed the detonator while Luke's bullets razed through his body. The RDX Khalid's men had laid out on the third floor went berserk.

▭

In the Situation Room, the screen went blank.

"What happened?" Hancock asked.

.  .  .

"We lost the connection."

They checked the news. There was a huge explosion on the third floor of the hospital. Huge bubbles of fire emanated out of that floor.

Hancock looked pale. He didn't know what to do now. He had hugely underestimated the shooters and now had multiple casualties on his head. He collapsed on his chair, his eyes staring blankly at nothing at all. An almost similar reaction was happening all across the room and across the nation.

# CHAPTER 43

HELMS HAD RECEIVED the call on his personal number from Riley, Sam Wick's handler, half an hour ago. She apprised him of the situation with Wick and Eddie. They were already airborne and now it was Helms' responsibility to clear the obstacles for them to help them enter American airspace.

━━

Sam Wick kept a watch on the first officer as he sat strapped to his seat. Eddie was in the first officer's seat, keeping an eye on the Captain. His instructions were to reach Houston as soon as possible.

He hoped that after nine hours of journey he would get the good news that the attacks had been contained, but he knew he had a streak of facing the worst of situations whenever he hoped for anything good.

.   .   .

Since the time he read those news reports, he had been analyzing the modus operandi of the attack. And he had come to an understanding that these men had arrived with extensive training and planning. Hitting six cities in broad daylight showed that.

Basit was still unconscious. The medicines might have been wearing off, but his hands and legs were cuffed, and he was strapped to a seat.

"We are in the US Airspace and heading to Houston now," the captain announced on the microphone. He had reluctantly agreed to fly the plane on the condition that his yes would save his crew.

Wick didn't react to the announcement. His eyes focused steadily on the three others. He had checked his watch for the fiftieth time in the last ten minutes. Sitting idle in the aircraft was no less than a torture, but at the same time, Wick was constantly planning what he had to do once they landed. Back home, the FBI and CIA had the prerogative to handle any terrorist threats. TF-77's role was curtailed once the message was delivered but Wick knew he might be needed.

'Couple of hours more,' Wick whispered to himself in the false hope of normalizing his nerves.

# CHAPTER 44

## WHITE HOUSE, **DC**

General Ronald Neller was staring at the door of the Situation Room with every inch of focus that he had in his body. He expected the door to open anytime soon, but he was surprised at the delay. He checked the time. It was nine pm. Almost eleven hours since the attack began, and it was still continuing. The reports from Manhattan were devastating. They had lost brave men and several innocent people in that raid. The terrorists were dead but the hospital building was completely aflame. He didn't know how long it would take to douse the fire.

"What the fuck are they waiting for?" General Neller muttered under his breath.

Master Sergeant David Blake was pacing back and forth in the hangar. Fifteen commandos, standing in a group at the far end of the hangar, waited for his orders. These men belonged to the United States Marine Corps Forces Special Operations Command (MARSOC). This was a component command of the United States Special Operations Command that comprised the Marine Corps' contribution to SOCOM. Its core capabilities were direct action, special reconnaissance and foreign internal defense along with conducting counterterrorism, and information operations.

David Blake, the stocky thirty-two-year-old, was a ten-year veteran of the Marines and one of the most respected and decorated noncommissioned officers in the entire MARSOC.

He and his team had arrived in Houston five hours ago, but they had orders not to leave the hangar without General Neller's order. Whatever was happening in Houston was their area of expertise, yet no one had called them. So, all they could do was wait and watch the news.

It was almost eleven at night when Blake got a call from General Neller, "Blake, we've been called. Make us proud."

"We will, sir," Blake said it with absolute sincerity.

"I'm waiting for the good news. All the best."

. . .

"Thank you, sir."

Blake looked at his men. They all were ready and raring to go. Not even one of them looked unsure or tired. This was what he wanted from his men, that was why he had personally been involved in their selection to his team. It wasn't as if someone gave these men to him and asked him to lead them. It was his team, and he had been the reason why these fifteen men were there. Looking at them, he felt responsible and proud.

They were stationed just eight miles off the city. He signaled the drivers to ready the SUVs.

"Team," Blake shouted. The fifteen men instantly looked at him. "Its time," he said.

The team ran onto the concrete road towards the vehicles. Each commando was carrying over thirty pounds of gear. For each of the commandos, this was the most important mission of his life. His trial by fire. They were armed with 9 mm semi-automatic Glocks holstered on their thighs. Heckler and Koch MP5 sub-machine guns and HK 416 completed the rest of the ensemble. Stun and fragmentation grenades bulged in the pouches of their bulletproof Kevlar vests over army combat fatigues. The Kevlar had two hard armor panels in the sleeves both in the front and the back of the jacket to protect against Kalashnikov bullets. Night vision goggles rested on their helmets.

Blake looked at his men as they settled in the vehicles. The information was still scarce and trickling in painfully slowly. The team only knew that there were seven to eight terrorists in the hotel but there was no information on the number of hostages. All they knew that it was on American soil and it was the biggest reason to act now, more than anything else.

# CHAPTER 45

WICK AND EDDIE rushed to the door as soon as the plane touched the runway. Outside, two black Suburban SUVs were already waiting for them. Jessica and Mac stood in somber silence near the first SUV, waiting for the jet to come to a halt. Three suits stood near the second Suburban, waiting to take Basit into their custody.

"Thank you, officers," Jessica said as soon as the suits put Basit in the Suburban. The men nodded their heads and without saying a word turned around. Jessica then looked at Wick, and as soon as his eyes met hers, he knew something was wrong.

"We need to go," Jessica said, before he could ask anything.

Inside the SUV, Wick found a new face alongside Mac. Stan was missing, but he said nothing. He wanted to know more before asking any questions. As soon as the SUV rolled on the concrete, Jessica took the onus on herself to explain what had happened in the last ten hours.

"Your information was correct," she said. "Six cities were hit this morning between 10 and 11 am. More than five thousand are dead, and the number is still rising with every hour as more and more bodies are being recovered from the debris. The attack on Philadelphia is neutralized, Manhattan is also free after a bloody fight. Houston is a different story. Terrorists have taken over the Onyx at the Marina and have been inside for more than nine hours."

"Where are we going?" Wick asked.

"Helms has a plan, but it will not fly without you."

"Does the President know about this?"

"No, he had shut Helms out from the proceedings in the Situation Room."

"What the hell? Has he gone mad?" Eddie said.

"I don't know what's in his mind. He still thinks that he is dealing with amateurs. His indecision had cost us a lot of time and now we are far behind in our response."

"Do you have a blueprint of the hotel?" Wick asked.

Mac knew this would come up. He rolled out multiple land-scape-sized printouts in the cramped space of the SUV. They all peered over the pages for the next ten minutes while Mac explained the various entry points of the hotel.

"What's the current situation of the target?" Wick asked.

"The terrorists have set afire the hotel roof and its top two floors. The fire department is not able to do anything about it due to the fear of getting shot at. The building is completely shut down."

"What about their demands?"

"None so far."

"Where's Stan?" Wick finally asked.

Jessica and Mac looked at each other. They didn't know how to say this. Mac finally decided to tell him. Wick's reaction was of pure shock and sadness. He and Stan had worked together on more than one occasion. He was a good soldier and a great man. No one spoke for a long time. Wick stared out of the window. His teeth clenched.

＝

Helms was waiting for the team a block away from the American General Center. As soon as the SUV came to a stop near him, Helms got in.

Wick looked at him. Helms looked tired, with bags under his eyes. He seemed genuinely relieved at finding Wick and Eddie in one piece. The SUV moved towards the American General Center.

"Sam and Eddie, thank you." Helms started with the one thing he wanted to say in person from the moment Wick and Eddie had agreed to go ahead with the suicide mission of getting Josh Fletcher out of the Taliban stronghold.

"Thank you, sir, but yesterday is old news. Why are we here?" Eddie said.

Wick just kept a straight face, hiding the storm brewing inside him since he heard about Stan.

"What I am going to ask you is dangerous and will have long-term repercussions, but we are left with no other choices. So, if any of you do not want to go ahead with what I am going to ask you to do, you can just open the door and leave."

"No matter what, I'm in, sir," Jessica spoke before anyone else. She had decided to go ahead with whatever hair-brained plan Helms had to kill those bastards. This was personal for her, more than others.

"Thank you, Jessica, but I'd still prefer it if you would hear what's ahead for you. As per my sources in the White House, the terrorists have not put forth any demands. That could only mean two things. Either they are waiting for something before they tell us what they intend to do with the hostages, or they simply don't have any demands. In the second scenario, the situation is more terrifying. No demands mean they probably will kill everyone and may take the whole building down with them. I tried to explain this to Hancock, but he is not listening to anyone except Walter Raborn, and Raborn is somehow convinced that they will call. With me telling you all this, we are already in grey territory and if we proceed to take things into our hands, then this will definitely be considered as a crime of the highest degree. I'm already at my retirement age and I can live with this blot for the rest of my life but all of you have a long career and life ahead so asking you to sacrifice everything on my wish is selfish and wrong."

He paused and spoke again, "Now I ask again, think about your options and if you want to leave it from here, you are welcome. No hard feelings." Helms looked at them, evaluating the five faces.

"I'm in," Jessica repeated her stance.

"Me too." Mac was second.

"Count me in too." Eddie was third.

"I'm in, sir." The guy whom Wick was not yet introduced to, was the fourth.

They all looked at Wick, who was still silent. "I need to talk to you in private," he said, looking at Helms. He opened his side of the door and got out. Helms looked uneasily at the rest of the crew and then followed Wick's lead.

Wick walked till he was at a respectable distance from the SUV. He turned around and found the NSA Director walking behind him. In the bright street light, Wick observed Helms carefully. His shoulders slouched, his walk was slow, and his face lacked its usual charisma. This was not the Helms Wick had known all these years.

"What's going on?" Wick directly cut to the chase when Helms was a comfortable distance from him.

.  .  .

"What do you mean?"

"I can understand your frustration with Hancock and Raborn but there is something that you are not telling us."

Helms stared at Wick for a moment longer. His face was blank. Helms didn't know how his own face looked right now. Was he so obvious? Was he losing his grip? Maybe he was getting too old that people could now read him like an open book.

"Where is Olivia?" Wick asked. He knew Olivia was doing an internship in the Onyx. He didn't know which division of the Onyx.

"How do you...?" Helms let the question disappear in the air. He was surprised at Wick's awareness. How did he know this? All he understood was that it was futile to hide his situation from Wick. "She is in the hotel."

"Onyx?"

.  .  .

"Yes."

"Alive?"

"Not sure. Her number is not reachable."

"Last contact?"

"Eight hours ago."

"Is this why you want this crack team?"

"No," Helms retorted.

"What if she's dead?"

"It's a possibility." Helms was slowly finding his composure. The steely determination in Wick's eyes was giving him strength too. From the moment he had heard Olivia's and Martha's voices on the phone, he had been emotionally unhinged. Now he felt as if he was getting back into his element.

. . .

"What if she is alive but dies in the skirmish?"

"I have thought about it. The priority is to save most of the hostages."

"You know, no one can guarantee a win here," Wick said.

"I know."

"What's the plan?"

Helms signaled at the American General Center. "There is a chopper waiting at the top of this building. I have pulled some strings to get special permission for it to fly despite restrictions in air traffic. It will take you to the top of the Onyx. Because of the fire, that is probably the only place where the terrorists are not looking. You will find five bags with the required ammo, Kevlar vests and fireproof clothes at the helipad."

Despite age, Helms had not lost his sharpness. Wick had thought of the same strategy while going over the blueprints with Mac.

"Who is the new guy?" he asked without betraying his emotions.

.   .   .

"Landon, he is one of the best marksmen, has four years of field experience and he has volunteered for the mission."

"You trust him?" Wick asked.

Helms nodded. "Will you do it?" he asked.

"I cannot tell you that. You will walk two blocks in that direction." He pointed in the direction of going away from the hotel. "You will not look back. You will take a cab to the airport and take the jet that brought you here. Your wife needs you. You need to tell her the situation and get her prepared for every eventuality. You will not watch TV; you will not go to the Internet. You will not try to find out anything about the mission until someone calls you and asks you about it. Then you will deny any knowledge of this mission. Can you do that?"

Helms nodded his head. He could've said no but something inside him told him to do what Wick was telling him to do. Maybe he was too blinded by his own emotions and he needed to get away from all this to collect his thoughts and focus on the next course of actions.

Wick saw Helms turning around and walking away. He stared at him for a few minutes. From the inside of the SUV, everyone was looking at the proceedings. They could not hear anything but by the look of it, Wick had convinced Helms to walk away for some strange reason.

Was the mission abandoned?

# CHAPTER 46

WICK WALKED BACK to the SUV and pulled the door open. Jessica, Landon, Mac and Eddie stared at him.

"Helms won't be coming back. We are going ahead with the mission but if any of us is captured or killed in the mission, he cannot be linked to us. It's time to cast your vote again. If anyone is changing his or her mind, he or she can leave."

No one said anything so Wick continued. "Jessica, what do you know about the chopper?"

"Helms pulled out some favors to get one," she replied.

"What about the blueprints? How well do you understand them?"

.  .  .

"We know our way around," Landon spoke.

"Two teams. Jessica and I; Eddie and Landon. Got it."

They nodded.

"Jessica you will lead our pair. Landon, you will lead yours. You guys know your way around as you have had more time to study the blueprints. Eddie and I will learn on the job. Once we are in, we will see how it pans out. Mac, you will help us navigate through the hotel."

"I knew it would come down to this," Mac said. He grabbed his bag and took out four tiny wireless tracking devices and a programmed master key to unlock any hotel room.

———

The four of them took the elevator to the roof of the American General Center building. Jessica led the way to the helipad at the roof. She walked in first, followed by Landon, Eddie, and Wick. Mac waited in the SUV parked in a parking lot, a couple of blocks away from the complex, connected with them through the wireless earpiece.

"Captain Marc Anthony." A man standing in front of a ten-million-dollar bird gave a crisp salute to the team.

·　·　·

"Thank you, Captain, for your help." Landon came forward to shake his hand.

"It's my duty to serve my country whenever required. These bags are for you." Marc gestured at four bags sitting comfortably near the helipad. Everyone instinctively moved forward to grab the bags. "Don't worry, I have not looked at what's in them," Marc spoke from behind.

Each bag had two Glocks, seven magazines, and a Heckler & Koch MP5 submachine gun. Wick liked the MP5s, since unlike AK-47s, their bullets did not ricochet. Kevlar vests, fireproof fatigues to cover their clothing, explosives, balaclava helmets, night vision glasses, grenades and satellite phones, everything was there. But the most important thing was the several meters of special polyester abseil ropes designed for a rapid descent from the choppers along with the large oven-mitt-sized gloves. Without the gloves, the rope would shear the skin off their palms.

The pilot saw the four people getting kitted at a fast pace. In ten minutes, they were ready to go.

"Captain, one more thing, for security reasons we cannot disclose our identities. And this cannot leak to the media. Hope you have no problem with that." Landon said.

.   .   .

"I understand."

"Let's go," Jessica ordered the captain.

On her orders, the two Safran Ariel 2C2 turbine engines of the Airbus H155 started to warm up and the five carbon fiber blades started to lift the plane vertically.

Once in the air, they could see the weakened flames on the Onyx roof. That was where they would land. The plan was to make an immediate landing, creating an illusion that the chopper was just flying over the building on its way to its destination. If the plan succeeded, then the team would have the element of surprise on their side.

No one attempted to settle in the helicopter. The destination was not far, and the five-ton machine was soon hovering over the Onyx.

"Thanks, Captain." Landon smiled.

The special polyester abseil rope, tethered to a boom, came down fast. Then the four bodies slithered down. Wick was first, then Jessica, Eddie, and Landon last.

.  .  .

The roof was isolated. The militants had possibly thought that the fire on the two floors would be enough to keep this way of entry blocked. If that was the case, then the team would not find much resistance. But if the hoax didn't work out, they would soon be facing heavy enemy fire.

# CHAPTER 47

ONYX HOTEL, **The Marina, Houston**

Three SUVs made their way through the empty streets of Houston at a hundred miles per hour in near-total darkness. They screeched to a halt a block away from the Onyx. Sixteen highly trained and seasoned Marines were riding in those heavy vehicles. All of them wore body armor, knee and elbow pads, and a specialized cut-down helmet with night-vision goggles affixed in a pop-down, pop-up mode.

They carried an arsenal of weapons, ranging from pistols to shotguns, to sniping rifles, to light and heavy machine guns. None of them had bothered to bring silencers. Their presence would be known within seconds of their arrival, and once they hit the ground, there was a chance they'd need every extra bullet and grenade they could carry. They were heading directly into the thick of things.

· · ·

The situation was of life and death, but the sixteen men were used to it and every last one of them was eagerly anticipating the battle that lay ahead.

A voice crackled over their earpieces announcing that they were two blocks from the target. In the resulting flurry of activity, optic rifle sights, red laser dot pointers, and night-vision goggles or NVGs were turned on, gear was shifted, and those who weren't already cocked and locked did so. The men were soon going to be in a race against time to fight the trained enemies before they could build an offense.

Blake and his team had also been provided with the hotel blueprints but in such a short time, it was impossible to understand the hotel's complex layout and plan an effective operation. But Blake had agreed just because General Shelton asked personally for him and was relying heavily on him and his men. The sixteen troopers were being dropped into the middle of a hostile environment where they were guaranteed to draw heavy enemy fire.

As soon as his SUV came to a halt, Blake opened his side of the door and was off, his weapon up and trained. His men moved swiftly towards their target in their pre-planned positions without uttering a word. All sixteen were able to talk via a secure internal radio link consisting of an earpiece and lip mike, but any communication was to be kept to an absolute minimum.

.  .  .

As they approached the building on foot, Blake could feel the emptiness of the streets and hear the gunshots. He knew that the distinct sound could only be from the AK-47s. There was no sign of life at the hotel. The windows were draped with curtains, and lights were switched off. Reaching near the cordoned off area, he took out the hotel blueprints once again and then looked up at the massive hotel complex in frustration.

Their guide stood ready near the building. As soon as they loomed near the building, Ted, a security officer in the Onyx and now their point person, approached them. He was in the CCTV room on the first floor when he saw the gunmen walking out of the toilet of the hotel, shooting at everyone at the reception area. Then they moved towards the lift when Ted thought of leaving the premises through the fire exit.

"How many men?" Blake asked him.

"Initially they were two but then their numbers swelled."

"Can you give us an exact number?" Blake asked him to recall the images again.

"Eight to ten." Ted was not sure, but he gave it his best shot.

.  .  .

"Cable TV connections in the hotel, from where are they managed? Can they be disconnected?" Blake knew that the only way terrorists inside would be able to know if the commandos were venturing inside was through the news channels. In the race for TV ratings, the news channels had no idea the kind of damage they were doing to the rescue mission.

"It needs to be done from inside the building."

"Any other options?"

"I can try to call the cable company and they might help us suspend the feed."

"Do it now."

Ted opened his flip phone and called his guy in the cable company. He was at home after his shift ended but agreed to help.

"He is saying he needs twenty minutes." Ted looked at Blake while clutching the phone.

"Ask him to do it fast."

.  .  .

"Sure, sir." Ted repeated the request on the phone.

"Last thing, can you decipher this?" Blake gestured at the blueprint.

Ted looked closely at the printed paper. It took his untrained eyes a moment to decipher the blueprint but soon the hotel structure started to emerge in front of him. Taking the CCTV room, where he sat, he started to see the fire exits, lobbies, and the rooms.

Blake keenly observed the man. Would he be able to be of any help was the question, but he had no other available option.

# CHAPTER 48

ONYX HOTEL, **The Marina, Houston**

The main door of the Onyx was locked. The team's demo man rushed to the locked entrance and slapped two thin adhesive ribbon charges on it. He carefully linked them together with a loop of orange Primadet cord and stepped back, pressing his body up against the wall. "Breaching charge ready," he said.

Blake listened as the other two elements of his team checked in. and then gave the thumbs-up signal to his door breacher.

"Fire in the hole!"

. . .

The sixteen troopers in front of the building lowered their heads as the charges were tripped, blowing the door off its hinges. The point man already had the pin on his flash-bang grenade pulled and wasted no time. He chucked the pyrotechnic through the open, smoking doorway and yelled, "Flash bang away!"

Every trooper sealed his eyes shut in anticipation of the blinding white-hot light of the grenade. At the sound of the thunderous explosion, the team moved, storming the first floor in a well-orchestrated maneuver. The point man entered the hotel first and immediately swept the space to the right as the second man came in and swept it to the left. The reception was deserted. Slowly the sixteen men started to take positions in the reception area.

The sixteen men moved in tandem covering their flanks one after another. Multiple phone cameras and the live telecast of the MARSOC teams getting into the hotel gave Taliban handlers enough reason to make contact with the men in the hotel.

"The Marines are coming. Go for the cross position," the handler instructed Shahrukh, who knew what his handler was talking about. He instructed his men. On his orders, the two men guarding the tenth floor rushed to the second floor of the hotel to join the four already there.

.    .    .

Shahrukh's handler called him again. "The hostages are only useful as long as you can use them as a shield. If at any point of time, you feel threatened, don't saddle yourself with their burden." Shahrukh agreed.

Shahrukh and Yakub were in the ballroom. With them were five hostages, all blindfolded, and they could easily become a burden in a battle of bullets.

The six terrorists on the second floor had begun to prepare for the biggest test of their training. The 3,000 square feet room on the second floor soon started to look like a battle-field with couches, cabinets, and refrigerators in the form of barricades. Four of the terrorists then wedged themselves in the small spaces behind the blockades, with the barrels of the AK-47s peeking out.

Their eyes on the big screen, everyone in the Situation Room seemed tense, watching yet another attempt to free the Onyx.

Blake led his team of commandos on to the second floor. They carefully ascended the stairs as per Ted's direction. Ted was at the rear, behind the team. A commando reached for the door leading to the second floor's lobby and tossed a flash grenade inside. Bathed in a blinding yellow flash, the lobby lit up like Christmas.

. . .

The commandos moved forward carefully once the flash subsidized. The lobby was deserted. The men took up their positions. The silence was eerie, as if someone already knew of their arrival. Sweeping their MP5s in front, they walked towards the first set of doors. The commandos padded noiselessly down the hall in single file, two feet apart, slightly crouched.

"There is an open door here," the commando leading the file hissed on his microphone.

Blake, who was third in line, looked in the direction. A sliver of light from the room spilled on to the hall. He signaled others to wait, with his right fist.

They tossed in another flash grenade and swiftly entered the room, their weapons covering the room from corner to corner. The space was clear.

A distinctive click. Someone had bolted a door in the lobby. Blake quickly came out of the room and saw his commandos watching the third door to their right.

He signaled one of his commandos to check the door. The commando moved forward, using the cover of the wall and gently turned the doorknob clockwise.

. . .

Locked. Stillness.

Blake signaled another one of his commandos, the door breacher. "Blast it," he said.

The man walked to the door and placed a pole charge on the door. As the commandos moved back, the demo man expertly drew an electrical wire and drew it till the end of the corridor. The commandos tensed themselves along the corridor, weapons ready. The demo man hooked the wire to a simple battery that he pulled out of his pocket. An electric current surged through the wire into the detonator. The deafening sound of the door blowing away into pieces rocked the corridor.

In normal circumstances, they'd have thrown grenades into the room first, but these were not normal circumstances. There could be hostages in the room. So, even before the smoke had settled, the commandos charged in through the splintered door. Four AK-47s opened up from inside.

Crack! Crack! Crack!

The first two commandos collapsed on the floor just outside the door. The terrorists had a small target to shoot at; the commandos were going in blind.

. . .

Next to cross the threshold, and roll down the corridor, was a grenade. The blast was earth-shattering. The other commandos immediately withdrew.

In the ballroom, Shahrukh heard the disjointed exchange of gunfire with concern.

So did Wick, Jessica and everyone else in the team who were still on the top floor.

A sharp crack of the Kalashnikovs and muted sound of MP5s.

"We've been hit. We've been hit. Commandos down." Blake heard these words, but in the melee of smoke, dust, and gunfire, it wasn't clear who was saying this, and who was hit and where. Blake waved his hand to clear the air. He saw three more commandos on the ground, bathed in a pool of blood. His heart sank. He knew who the three bodies were.

Just over thirty minutes into the operation and they had suffered a serious setback. Casualties were unacceptable in a seek-and-destroy mission.

. . .

In the confusion, no one had noticed that a door behind the MARSOC unit was opened and two shooters had snuck into the second-floor lobby through the back stairs without making a sound, waiting for their chance at the bend.

The commandos retreated away from the door, towards the stairs from where they had entered the lobby when two AK-47s had gone mad.

The commandos were not ready for a major fire from behind. The lobby was long and plain. There was no place to take cover. Two more commandos took the bullets on their backs and one got hit on his leg. The rest of the men turned around to face the two shooters and shot blindly. Blake who had been at the front, was now at the back as the battlefield was turned one hundred and eighty degrees. The low-velocity MP5 bullets raced to find their targets but they neither had the velocity nor the incisive power to penetrate the hallway parapets behind which the terrorists took cover. The bullets from the enemy had no such barriers.

For the first time in his life, Blake felt helpless. The enemy was fast and agile. There was no time to reorganize the team against the assault.

"Grenades, throw grenades," Blake shouted.

.  .  .

However, the terrorists acted first. A hand grenade sailed out from the bend and landed in the lobby near the dead bodies of the first line of commandos. The rest of the men had less than 3 seconds to react. They all moved back, but the retreat was not fast enough. The grenade exploded with an ear-splitting blast. It peppered the two first-in-line commandos with steel ball bearings. Blood, flesh, smoke, and dust.

The four terrorists holed up in the room suddenly sprang into action, leaving their safety nets. They felt the waves of the blast in their rooms and a balloon of dust rising. Their guns aimed at the broken door.

Blake and his men were now jammed in between the two shooting teams. The tables had turned, and Blake was acutely aware that his team's chances had dropped severely. Seven commandos were still alive but one of them was badly hurt. Six men against six terrorists. The commandos had to regroup quickly if they were to survive. Blake spoke into his lip-mic and his men quickly re-organized in two teams, of four and two, facing opposite directions.

Blake led the team of four who would be taking on the terrorists in the room. The second team, that had two Marines, faced the other side. After a pause of a couple of minutes, Blake fired four tear gas canisters into the room. At the other side of the lobby, two grenades flew in the direction of the shooters. The two terrorists behind the bend had already expected this and had taken cover. Inside the room, amidst the bullets and tear gas, the four terrorists felt the noose tightening. The 3,000 square feet room had suddenly started to shrink. Death seemed very real. They all looked at each other and found the fear each of them felt reflecting on the other faces as well.

Two Marines decided to flank the room from the other side. They paused at the edge of the open door and then quickly jumped the space to get to the safety of the wall.

The militants saw shadows in the smoke and pressed their triggers. Bullets raced to the door to meet flesh and blood.

The commandos heard the crackling assault rifles and tried to speed up, but a couple of stray bullets still found their way into one Marine's calf muscle. The other one just got lucky.

The Marine duo covering the opposite side of the hallway slowly moved towards the bend. They could not wait for the two shooters to disappear into the building.

They rapidly moved forwards in the dust and smoke, taking up positions. Crossing the bend, they found another straight hallway at the end of which stood a shadow. As soon as the silhouette spotted the Marines, he started firing. They took cover and retaliated. The silhouette took advantage of this momentary break and disappeared again. When the Marine duo checked the hallway, it was vacant. They signaled each other and the two of them rushed towards the spot.

Visibility was still low. Fifty yards in the corridor, the first Marine had to stop. He had accidentally tripped a booby trap with his foot and it only meant one thing.

⊏══⊐

One of the Marines had thrown two grenades in the hotel room when the blast in the adjacent corridor shook the floor.

Blake was two men down. His own situation wasn't good either. His ears were ringing and his brain was numb.

In the room, the four terrorists were now three. The two grenade blasts in the room had taken the life of one. These three  had to now find a way to get out of the mess. They decided to shoot their way out of it.

In the hallway, three distinct gunshots came from the room. And two distinct footsteps from across the bend, coming for them. Blake looked at his men. There was no way they were going to get out of there alive.

.   .   .

"Cap, we will fight to the death." Blake saw one of the injured Marines trying to get up. The other injured Marine had decided to step up too. Including Blake, they were a total of five men still standing amidst the massacre.

# CHAPTER 49

ONYX HOTEL, **The Marina, Houston**

Mac was glued to his laptop's screen. He saw four bright dots, one over another. The team had landed on the roof.

"Everything good?" Mac hissed in the earpiece.

"Yes, what next?" Jessica asked.

"You will find a door somewhere to your left. That's your entry." Mac's job as a guide had begun.

"What's happening?" Wick asked as he heard the sound of bullets in the building.

. . .

"As per the internet live feeds, there is a battle going on at the second floor. A MARSOC team was seen to be going in thirty minutes earlier."

"You can watch this on the Internet?" Wick was surprised.

"Yes, people with mobile cameras are live feeding this on their social media channels."

"I thought there was a media blanket on covering this."

"Yes, but on social media, people post all kind of shit."

"Bloody hell. If we can see it, then the terrorist handlers can also watch it and alert their men in the building. Can you check if there is any live feed about us landing on the roof?"

"Okay, but it will take some time."

"Do it fast, I need to know if the enemy knows that we are here."

Twenty minutes later, Mac came back with an answer. No one had expected anyone to land at the burning floor, so no camera was pointed at it after it was done burning for several hours.

# CHAPTER 50

ONYX HOTEL, **The Marina, Houston**

Blake and his men now stood in the hallway facing both sides. Let the enemy come for them rather than the other way around.

The shots from the bend had started again, hitting the concrete wall but this time Blake and his men had a different strategy. Their weapons were reloaded, and they waited patiently amidst the falling concrete, for the enemy to appear.

The absence of response from the Marines gave the two terrorist teams, in the hallway and inside the room, a false sense of security. And then they made their first two mistakes in quick succession.

. . .

The first mistake was that the two terrorists across the bend decided to venture away from their cover positions. In their over-confidence, one of the two in the hallway left his cover and ventured out, looking for the Marines. Behind him was his partner. The lobby still had almost no visibility.

From their crouched positions, the two Marines saw the two silhouettes appearing in the open and pressed their triggers. Headshots. Both. Two bodies hit the floor in quick successions. Silence followed.

The three terrorists in the room looked at each other, surprised at the sudden burst of firing. As if someone had pulled the plug from a heavy metal concert. They waited for any retaliatory fire.

In the ballroom, Shahrukh felt as if the tremors had stopped. He spoke to the terrorist holed up inside the room. "Nawaz, what's the situation?"

"I don't know. There isn't any fire from the commandos."

"Are they dead?"

"Not sure. We are inside the room. Outside visibility is almost non-existent." Nawaz was telling the truth.

.  .  .

"What about Aslam and Mir?" Shahrukh asked, referring to the two terrorists who had been shooting from behind the bend.

"I'm not sure. They might be injured. Not able to contact them."

"Wait for a few minutes, let the dust settle and then look out for them."

"Okay."

Ten more minutes. Nothing happened. No movement in the lobby. Blake and his men had now retreated into the hallway. If anyone ventured out, the first impression he would get would be a vacant hallway peppered with dead Marines all around. The terrorists didn't know how many Marines were in the hallway initially, so Blake's team had the element of surprise with them now. They waited.

▭

Everyone in the Situation Room was waiting too.

▭

Inside the room, the silence was turning unbearable for the three terrorists. Blake and his team were suddenly playing with the terrorist's fear of inaction. Nawaz eventually signaled the other two terrorists to check the lobby but not from the main door. Every suite in the Onyx had two doors. In the case of this room, both doors opened in the same lobby but were at two ends.

The terrorists were talking about taking the second exit. The three of them moved in tandem towards the door, two at the front and Nawaz at the back. The important thing was to open the door noiselessly. The doorknob rotated clockwise and freed the door.

Blake heard the click sound first and saw the wooden door moving. The surprise of finding another exit was soon over-come by the thought that the terrorists had decided to take this exit. He touched the shoulders of the Marine standing next to him to let him know about the new development. Slowly the five Marines positioned themselves around the door, their backs against the wall.

The door opened and the first terrorist ventured out, followed closely by the second. The first terrorist turned to his right and found a man in a black helmet staring at him, his MP5 pointing at his abdomen. The second terrorist saw it a second late and tried to get back into the room, but two MP5s roared and bullets pierced through the bodies of the two terrorists at supersonic speed. The two of them fumbled while trying to get back in the room but their bodies refused to go anywhere.

.    .    .

Nawaz, who was just behind the two, saw his people going down and started firing blindly. His AK-47 peppered the small entry point with bullets. The Marines had expected this and had already taken cover.

In his fearful rage Nawaz had forgotten that even the AK-47 needs a reload. As soon as he paused, Blake and his men stormed inside the room, their MP5s trained in Nawaz's direction and firing. Nawaz was in the middle of reloading his weapon when the bullets met him. He was dead before he hit the floor. The three un-injured Marines quickly got in the suite to check for any other terrorists.

They found one more militant's dead body near the bed.

⸻

"Mac, can you check  the status on the second floor?" Wick asked.

"I'm not sure how. The CCTVs can only be navigated by getting into the control room that is somewhere on the first or second floor. Hacking it will take more time."

"It's better if we ask Helms to get the updates from the Situation Room." Wick told Jessica.

"Okay, let me talk to him." Jessica offered.

In the Situation Room, several eyes smiled as their best men finally won a hard-fought battle. But this victory came at the price of losing eleven of them. A medics team was on on the way, with Ted's help, to tend to the injured Marines.

General Shelton and General Neller looked dumbfounded and angry at the same time. They had not expected the terrorists to be so well-trained. They were just mercenaries and against them were America's best men. It was unprecedented in the history of the MARSOC teams. Never had they faced such an adversary where this team had to face *this* kind of resistance. But that day, many things had happened that no one had expected to happen.

## CHAPTER 51

ONYX HOTEL, **The Marina, Houston**

Helms' source told him about the six dead terrorists on the second floor and about the eleven martyred Marines. Reinforcement would take time and a new strategy had to be formulated now.

Jessica relayed this information to everyone else.

As per the estimate, Onyx housed eight to ten terrorists. Jessica and Wick's were sure that the remaining terrorists would try to fortify their positions, maybe by using hostages.

Onyx had thirty numbered floors but in reality, it only had twenty-nine floors. This was because like most hotels, Onyx didn't have a thirteenth floor. The building had three entry or exit points. These were at the lobby level, at the pool level, and a route that not many knew – from the second basement all up to the thirtieth floor, used for maintenance. The team hoped that the terrorists were only aware of the lobby and the pool stairs and not the one used for maintenance. If that was the case, then this was the only route to find them and kill them.

"What's the plan?" Landon asked. They were on the twenty-eighth floor right then.

"We need to get to the floor where the remaining terrorists are holding up." Jessica said.

"That means checking each room on each floor," said Wick. There wasn't any other option.

Jessica, MP5 in her right hand, gingerly opened the door of the faintly lit stairwell. The hotel's emergency fire exit spiraled down to the second basement. Behind her was Wick. Landon and Eddie followed.

They were still not sure if they would find any terrorist on this route, but it was the best option they had. They had switched off their earphones for the time being to do away with any distractions.

. . .

Jessica and Wick moved down, holding one side of the stairs, and covering the corridor with their weapons. Then, Landon and Eddie leapfrogged them.

The fire-escape door on the twenty-seventh floor had push bars, which meant that it could be opened only from the hotel corridor, and not from the fire escape. A force sneaking up the fire escape would have no option but to break the door down and give itself away. They decided to try the next floor.

Finally, on the twentieth floor, they saw a crack in the fire escape door. It was slightly ajar, wide enough to stick a knife blade in.

In the lobby, a macabre trail led them to the spot of a fresh slaughter. Scattered bullet holes on the ceiling of the stairs. Then, a pair of broken spectacles. A shoe. A lady's slipper. A silk scarf leading them upstairs. The four of them slowed down, then stopped altogether when they looked up. A bloodied hand hung limply from the staircase.

The twentieth floor also opened to a two-level elevator machinery room. The stairs telescoped into an iron ladder barely four feet wide and six feet long. There were rivulets of blood running down from the stairs above. Six bodies were heaped on top of each other. The terrorists had executed their hostages at point-blank range. There were bullet holes on the wall, and bullets had knocked the light bulb out. The door was locked. There was no point in blasting the door down. It was a dead end.

They decided to try another route. Finally, they found the spot from where they could see the complete cavernous polygonal atrium of the Onyx. Over thirty rooms per floor were wrapped around this vertiginous space. The fiberglass skylight was letting the moonlight into the atrium. Standing there, the layout of the hotel became clearer to the team. If you treated the atrium as the face of a clock, there were three entry points onto each floor: fire exit stairs at five and ten o'clock and a set of service stairs behind the elevators at eight o'clock. They had entered on to the twentieth floor from the fire escape. Now they moved clockwise around the corridor and circled the atrium as they headed for the service stairs at eight o'clock that led straight to the next floor.

There was an eerie, muffled silence in the atrium, the silence that terror and the fear of death will bring. Nothing else was out of place. All the polished brown doors that led to the rooms were shut. Each floor had a three-foot-high wall that ran around the central space, made alternately of brick and glass partitions, the latter having tubular brass balustrades.

They four of them looked across the floor where they could see most of the rooms on their level and below. In a tactical situation, such a commanding view leveled the playing field between them and the terrorists. The black figures filed quietly along the red-carpeted floor, briefly merging with the black granite cladding of the elevator area.

And then Wick saw Shahrukh, hastily walking near the pool with an AK-47 in his hand. He was looking up.

"Fall back," Wick hissed and all of them simultaneously reacted.

Shahrukh pushed the two hostages inside the room. Yakub checked the lobby on the seventh floor and closed the door from inside.

"Sit!" Yakub ordered the two Americans who were already too scared to protest.

They had chosen two people from the ballroom hostages whom they felt could be easily handled and were less of a flight risk. One was a young girl of roughly the same age as Shahrukh and Yakub, in her early twenties, and other was a middle-aged man. Both were injured and that was why they were not a flight risk and posed a lesser threat to Yakub and Shahrukh. They had found the girl in the second floor's ballroom, hiding among the dead. Her name was Olivia and she was a hotel employee. The other hostage was Peter Jacob, who worked for a multinational firm and was staying in the hotel for the last two days for business meetings. They both looked shell-shocked.

The death of six of their colleagues had shaken Shahrukh and Yakub too. The two of them now had to stay together to remain alive.

Five minutes later, Shahrukh got a call from the handler. "How are things?"

"Only Yakub and I are alive," Shahrukh said.

"Where are you both?"

"In room 0724 with two hostages."

The handler thought for a moment about the situation. "What are their names?" he asked.

"Olivia Helms and Peter Jacob," Shahrukh responded.

"They will send reinforcements, but it will take some time. Keep in mind that the hostages are of use only as long as you don't come under fire, because America weighs their safety more. If your lives are threatened, then don't saddle yourself with the burden of the hostages. Immediately shoot them."

"We understand."

"Remember, every nation prefers to claim that no hostages were harmed during their operations. That everyone was saved. So, use their weakness to your advantage. And stay alert."

"We will."

And the line was disconnected.

# CHAPTER 52

ONYX HOTEL, **The Marina, Houston**

"Mac, which floor has the pool?" Wick asked as soon his comms were switched on.

"Seventh," Mac said.

"There is a shooter near the pool. We need to move fast." Wick instructed the others.

They nodded. They walked in pairs, through the narrow passage behind the elevators on the nineteenth floor. At the beginning of the eighteenth floor, they discovered the bodies of three women hostages laid out in a triangular formation. They did not move the bodies for fear of booby traps, and just crossed over them carefully.

. . .

As they kept moving down, sweeping every floor for terror-ists, their movements were soon fine-tuned to drill-like perfection. For opening any door, they used the master key given to them by Mac. As soon as the LED in the automatic lock beeped green, the first person would shove the door wide open and point his weapon ahead into the room. This move would startle anyone hiding behind the door.

Room 0724, like any other room, had a brown wooden door with an oval brass number plate. It stood at the head of a narrow passage that led to five other rooms – 0721 through to the 0725 – that were hidden from view behind the guest elevators.

Wick drew the master key out of his pocket and inserted it into the key slot. The tiny LED light on the door lock blinked, turned green and beeped. He then shoved the door forward.

Crack! Crack!

A burst of two AK-47 bullets hammered the bottom of the door. Shahrukh had been standing behind the door, his rifle ready and cocked. Wick had startled him. As Shahrukh fell back, his bullets punched and splintered the door. A bullet grazed Wick's right arm. He quickly backed off and took cover with his back pressed to the wall.

.  .  .

The sound of the shots ripped across the atrium. Shahrukh and Yakub kept up the intensity, and the shooting continued.

Instinctively, the others spread out. The four of them covered various parts of the polygonal floor. Jessica covered the area closest to the bank of elevators near the room; Eddie stood in the corridor to the right; Landon covered the corridor across the atrium. Wick was still the one closest to the room. All their weapons pointed at Room 0724.

Shahrukh and Yakub's bullets whistled and cracked across the corridor as they broke the sound barrier. Across the atrium, Landon took shelter behind a four-foot-high wooden table used to hold flowers. Intermittently, he raised his head to fire a few shots at the room. Just then, he heard the crack of a bullet as it whizzed past and felt the sensation of a hard slap. The bullet had split his ear in two. His ear went numb. Blood poured onto his black t-shirt. He cupped his left hand over his ear... it was filled with blood.

"Fuck," Eddie shouted, "You are bleeding."

"You expected water?" Landon said dryly. With that, he pulled out a white field-dressing pack out of his pocket and put it on his ear. The white bandages quickly turned red.

.  .  .

Meanwhile, the fusillade of bullets from the room had bent the brass balustrade and shattered the glass below it. The terrorists were cornered, but they would not go down without a fight. They opened the door of the room to fire and tossed grenades at the enemy. Their 'fire discipline' surprised Wick and others. The two men inside fired only single shots, and they kept jockeying their firing position. Any two shots rarely came from the same location. Their room was a defender's delight, a natural pillbox that had evidently been chosen with care. It was set in the corner of a corridor, protected by the bulge of the elevators on the right. The door was set at least four feet inside the wall, protected by the rooms on the left.

Wick and others, on the other hand, had a restricted field of fire. That was why the terrorists had chosen the Onyx and not any other location for the siege. The Onyx, with its atrium and multiple exits, offered them many more options to battle it out. It was indeed a very well-thought-out operation.

## CHAPTER 53

IRFAN-UL-HAQUE – the Great Cleric – relayed the information he had received from Shahrukh's handler to the Professor who was in constant touch with him via a secure line.

"Who are the hostages?" Professor asked.

"Peter Jacobs and Olivia Helms," the Cleric told him.

"Kill them."

"But they might be helpful in making the siege longer." The Cleric was surprised.

. . .

"I will not repeat myself."

The Cleric didn't respond this time. He knew he had no other options than to comply.

———

The handler called Shahrukh again. "What's the situation?" he asked.

"There is already a team outside the room, firing at us. We are outnumbered."

"Get rid of the hostages."

"But..."

"Do it. I'm keeping on hold. Go on, do it, do it. I'm listening...do it." Shahrukh had to comply. He stared at Yakub with helplessness and shot Peter. Olivia shrieked. Getting up, she limped helplessly towards the door. Yakub took aim at her and before she could cross the door, multiple bullets riddled her body.

———

Wick had to lose his train of thought when he heard the shriek followed by gunshots. Someone was running towards them and before Wick could understand anything, Olivia's body flew out of the door. Her back had innumerable bullet holes and she hit the floor face down.

A grenade flew in close proximity to her and landed in the lobby. Wick jumped without waiting. The grenade exploded in mid-air. Steel splinters rushed to meet Wick's body. By the time he landed, he knew many of them had found their way into his bullet-proof vest. Without it, he would have been dead meat.

This was getting out of hand. They had to blast open the door since the terrorists were easily able to open it, at will. They had to take away this control from them. Jessica ordered Landon and Eddie to provide her with covering fire. While she crawled closer to the room, Wick pulled Olivia's dead body away from the door. There was silence from inside; perhaps the terrorists had paused to reload their weapons.

Jessica placed the charge on the door, and the explosion managed to partially splinter it. As soon as the door was breached, Wick lobbed multiple grenades into the room. There was an ear-splitting explosion. The firing from within the room had begun, and it instantly subsided. Jessica and Wick kept lobbing stun grenades into the room. Landon and Eddie kept up the pressure with intermittent cover fire. The firefight was slowly tilting towards Wick's team. The dull subsonic sounds of the MP5, like a coconut hitting the floor, versus the AK-47's firecracker sound, echoed through the atrium.

In the incessant firing, Wick and Jessica didn't have the time to check if there were any hostages in the room.

In the hotel elsewhere, the guests cowered in fear.

# CHAPTER 54

LANDON AND EDDIE kept firing at the door to keep the terrorists from breaking out. But they had begun running low on ammunition. Jessica opened her bag and took out some Molotov cocktails. She lit them one by one and flung them at the door. The cocktails crashed through the gap in the door and set the room on fire. The curtains obscuring the view quickly burned away. Black smoke billowed out of the room. The fire also triggered off the hotel's sprinkler system. Water spurted out of spouts in the ceiling, extinguishing the fire. This gave them a clear view of the room from outside.

Shahrukh and Yakub rushed into the bathroom for shelter. Wick and Jessica lobbed more grenades into the room, but they proved futile. The terrorists opened the faucets in the bathroom. Water started to fill the bathtub, spreading out into the room and gushing into the corridor outside.

.   .   .

At the same time, Shahrukh and Yakub also had a conversation with their handlers who kept them at it with motivational speeches. "The manner of your death will instil fear in the unbelievers. This is a battle between Islam and the unbelievers. Keep looking for a place to die. Keep moving."

"Insha'allah," they responded earnestly.

"You're very close to Heaven now. One way or another we've all got to go there. You will be remembered for what you've done here. Fight till the end. Stretch it out as long as possible."

It was past midnight and Room 0724 and its vicinity resembled a coal pit. The fire had charred the whitewashed walls around the room. The corridor was indistinguishable from the black granite facade of the elevators. The firefight and the water had turned the area around the room into a slushy puddle. The grenade blasts had knocked the light fittings out in front of the room and lift area. They had also smashed the false ceiling to reveal a thick mass of black electrical cables. Cable TV routers and wires hung limply like creepers. The corridor filled with half an inch of water, turning the red carpet into a soaking bog.

What Jessica and Wick didn't know was that one of the grenade blasts had injured Yakub grievously. There was no way he could be saved.

While sitting in the van, Mac decided to make himself useful by tuning into the various frequencies, to see which of them were being used by the terrorists. Eventually, he succeeded in latching on to one. Mac captured their conversation on his device.

"How are you, my brother?" The handler asked them.

"Praise God. Yakub has passed away." Shahrukh sounded weak.

"Really? Is he there?"

"Yes."

"May God accept his martyrdom."

"I'm sitting in the bathroom with the taps on," Shahrukh said, looking at Yakub's dead body.

"Don't let them arrest you. Don't let them knock you out with a stun grenade. That would be very damaging. Fire one of your magazines, then grab the other one and move out. The success of your mission depends on you getting shot," the handler suggested.

———

"Jessica, one of them is dead. Only one is left." Mac hissed in his lip mic.

"How do you know?" she asked.

"Snooping on the frequency they are using to talk to their handlers. He is going to come out. He doesn't want to be captured."

"Thanks."

Eddie was on guard at the fire exit near five o'clock. Landon was with him. Wick was still near the door, with a four-foot-high housekeeping trolley next to him that stood shielding him from any shots from the room. He felt dazed and tired. The travel, firing, and explosions had numbed him. It was the thought of Stan that kept him going.

Jessica took stock of the situation. The four of them were tired, but she had to regroup them and launch another assault on the room.

. . .

Suddenly a short burst of fire echoed through the atrium. It was difficult to tell the location of it, but the gunfire did not come from within the room. It was in the atrium.

'Who's firing?' they wondered. Was it the MARSOCs or the SWAT Teams?

There was a second burst. This time very close to where Wick stood. The bullets drilled the wall and blasted out puffs of white dust. "Damn," Wick yelled as he darted back into the corridor for cover.

The figure fired again, this time from within the narrow niche of the elevator door. Still unsure about the identity of the shooter, Wick raised his MP5, but Jessica motioned him to hold back.

She shouted frantically. 'The man is in black. It could be one of ours.'

The figure continued to fire and move towards Eddie and Landon who quickly took cover. Wick shot a glance out of his cover. It was Shahrukh in black tees with his AK-47. He had taken advantage of the dark corridor and a lull in the fighting and broken out of the second door of the room opening into the lobby, determined to shoot his way out. Wick's thumb slipped his MP5 selector to a three-round burst, and he aimed and fired two quick bursts. The MP5 rattled.

Shahrukh was hit in the leg. He staggered and limped back towards the elevators.

Enraged, Shahrukh screamed, "You coward, why are you hiding? If you are worth your salt, come out and fight." He then ran for cover himself.

Eddie appeared from the shadows and took aim at the place where Shahrukh was hiding. Shahrukh was now being shot at from two different directions. Eddie shouted, "Now why don't you come forward?"

A tense stand-off ensued. Both held their positions. Eddie and Landon were almost out of ammo, and they informed Jessica and Wick about it. Now, the two of them had to stop Shahrukh from slipping out in the dark into the other side of the corridor.

Wick asked Eddie to go onto the next floor and fling grenades at Shahrukh's location from there. Wick wanted to create an illusion that Shahrukh was now trapped from all directions. Either he could surrender or die.

•  •  •

Wick and Jessica reloaded their weapons while Eddie ran up to the eighth floor. He had just two hand grenades left, and he had to make them count.

Shahrukh kept firing single shots, inaccurately, from his hideout in the elevator passageway, but he was now clearly out of his depth. Eddie positioned himself nearest to the place from where Shahrukh was firing and lobbed two grenades at it in quick succession. With the twin explosions, the firing stopped.

Wick threw a stun grenade into the atrium. And in the blinding light, he spotted the body of the dead terrorist lying in the corridor. He aimed his MP5 and fired one quick burst at the body. No movement. He walked down the corridor. Shahrukh lay inert on the floor, his dead eyes staring at Wick. His AK-47, five magazines and a pistol lay beside him. Empty cartridges lay scattered around.

Jessica swung open what was left of the door to Room 0724. It was a compact battle zone. The terrorists had used the room's two doors as a barrier. They had used the minibar and a study table as firing positions. She stepped on hundreds of AK-47 brass empties. The windows, the bed, and a sofa were half burned. The carpeted floor was soggy and strewn with shoes and clothes. She aimed her weapon at the bathroom. The door was open. A terrorist lay on his back on the bathroom floor. Shrapnel had passed through his right eye. This was Yakub.

. . .

Inside the room, Peter Jacob also lay dead.

Outside, Wick rolled over the dead body of the woman that lay in the corridor and immediately recognized her. She was Olivia Helms. He looked back at Eddie who looked shocked and disturbed. He knew who Olivia was.

⸻

The terrorists had been neutralized, but the operation did not end there. The MARSOC teams carried out room intervention operations in the rest of the hotel, moving from the top downwards.

The Onyx was eventually cleared of civilians. Bodies of the dead civilians were removed by the noon next day. Guests from all floors were thoroughly screened again and handed over to the hotel authorities. The bomb disposal squad conducted their Render Safe Procedure, sweeping the hotel for live ordnance and ammunition, and searching for possible booby traps before the building was handed over to the hotel authorities.

# CHAPTER 55

THE NEWS CHANNELS were awash with the news of victory over terror. Once again, they were trying to give the ominousness of the attacks a positive spin, but the people actually affected were the ones who knew that no amount of positivity could bring their loved ones back from the dead.

The dead were in thousands. In the absence of any official figures, the estimate game had already begun on various news channels. TV debates had already started, with hashtags and with quotes, in a bid to make them trend on social media. After the initial condemnations and sympathies from the politicians and public figures alike, the blame games had also started within the various stakeholders responsible to keep America safe.

Wick, Jessica, Eddie and Landon stood in silence as the medical teams rushed inside the Onyx to tend to the hostages. Wick had called Helms a few minutes ago to deliver the news of Olivia's death. It was one of the hardest things to do in life – letting a father know that his child was no more. Helms said nothing, he just listened to what Wick told him and then he disconnected the call.

In Manhattan, Richard survived, but the one person he wanted to live his life with finally succumbed to her injuries in the hospital. Richard kept holding Lily's hand long after she was gone.

In Philadelphia, Mary woke up to the news of her only son's martyrdom. The officer who gave her the news asked her if she had anyone whom he could call to be with her at this time. All she could was to stare at him blankly. She didn't even cry. She just sat there on that hospital bed; her mind blank. What would she do without her son? With whom would she go to the market?

# CHAPTER 56

HANCOCK'S first feeling was of relief. The immediate next thought was of the political fallout he was about to face. During his walk from the Situation Room to the Oval office, he met many people, and all of them congratulated him on the successful mission. But as soon as he closed the Oval office door, his fears roared back with vengeance. 'What would be tomorrow's headline? Would he be a hero for America?' he wondered.

Hancock's train of thought was interrupted only when his phone rang. It was Peter Jackson – his ex-Special Advisor who had quit his job moments before the attacks.

*'Finally, someone has realized his mistake to abandon the ship at the worst moment and is now eager to board it again,'* Hancock thought, while picking up the phone. An involuntary smile caressed his lips. If anyone could help him milk this opportunity to the fullest, it was Peter Jackson.

. . .

"Hello Pete," he said.

"Hello Mr. President." Jackson sounded earnest.

"Calling to congratulate me?"

"You deserve it, sir."

"I know," Hancock gloated. He pictured Jackson running his hand through his signature bleach-blond hair and smiled.

"You must be first President who not only thought of this impossible task but also executed it ruthlessly. And then, of course, saved the day for everyone." Jackson sniggered.

Hancock's voice shook. "What do you mean?"

"Isn't it crystal clear? I mean, you wanted me to do this but then you went ahead, got this done and that too on the same day."

. . .

"You are accusing me of..." Hancock suddenly stopped short of saying the exact words. His phone could be tapped by the Secret Service as protocol. He didn't know, because he had never cared until now.

"Am I? Do I sound like I'm accusing you of anything you are not capable of? You... the President of the United States? I only called to congratulate you on your glorious victory."

Hancock said nothing in return. He wanted to, but he didn't.

"And tomorrow when the whole world will revel in America's victory on terror, when you will be cherished and celebrated as the strong leader that this nation deserves, I will be the proudest of all because I made you the President. Not the people of this country, not the media, not your senators but I did. You know that, right?"

"Yes, Peter it's you. It will always be you." Hancock swerved around, changing his tactic.

"But Hancock, tell me, what did I get in return? A shitty designation, Special Advisor to the POTUS! What is that, a slap for good work?"

. . .

"Peter, why don't you come and meet me? We can talk...sort this thing out."

"I'd love to, but you see I don't have time for a President who is going to be impeached soon. Your time is over, buddy."

"You are threatening the President of this country!"

"I'm just saying that one should cover one's tracks more closely. In this age of trending hashtags, you can never tell when it's going to be your face on one of those viral videos."

"What do you mean?"

"Okay if you want it in simpler words, then let it be so. Hancock, you should have never said those things to me that you did in our last meeting." Jackson took a long sigh. "But you did. Don't worry, I will keep your golden words very safe with me." And with that, Jackson disconnected the call.

Hancock remained standing at his place, alone in the Oval office, looking into the darkness. His own words from that conversation, ringing louder in his ears.

.   .   .

"*Think about it, an attack on this country and people will forget about everything. This is what I need.*"

# CHAPTER 57

"THE MESSAGE IS DELIVERED." Jackson spoke on the phone.

"Good."

"Anything else for me?"

"Not now, but soon," the man said, speaking slowly.

"Thank you, Professor!"

And the phone was disconnected from the other end.

*The End.*

**—> *GET WICKED DEATH* <—**

*SAM WICK UNIVERSE THRILLER 8*

Thank you for reading my book. I hope you would have enjoyed it. Would you be interested in telling me your views on the story?

## LEAVE A REVIEW - USA
## LEAVE A REVIEW - UK
## LEAVE A REVIEW - AUSTRALIA
## LEAVE A REVIEW - CANADA
## GOODREADS

Book reviews are not only important to you as a readers, but they are critically important to authors like me. As a novelist, I can tell you that I depend heavily on reviews from my readers.

They not only help others to find my books, but more importantly, they help me to improve my craft so the next book I write will be even better.

Well I am here to urge you, dear reader, to leave book reviews either on Amazon, Goodreads or BookBub.

## Where you can write review on the Amazon book page

Click the links above and they will open the respective review pages of my book in your preferred Amazon store.

Click the button "Write a customer review" (Please note that the words might vary in your country's amazon store)

On clicking the button, you will be taken to a page where you can rate the book from 1 to 5 stars (5 being the highest) and you can write a couple of line about the book.

If you face any issues, please let me know at *chaseaustincreative@gmail.com* and I will be glad to help you with the process.

# YOUR FREE BOOKS

**Do not forget to download your FREE COPY of WICKED STORM & WICKED SHOT**

**Check: www.thechaseaustin.com**

# DEDICATION

To My Family

## ACKNOWLEDGMENTS

A big thanks to my **advance readers group** who are nothing but supportive of my writing**,** especially to **Janet Lerner, Alex Mellor, Terry Pigeon, Pat Manfield, Cath McTernan,** and **David Taylor** who are extremely helpful in rectifying mistakes that would have ruined the experience of reading this story.

A special shoutout to my Facebook group members who are always encouraging and patient with my infrequent Facebook outings and news about my new projects.

A special thanks to my Editor who stepped up to help me complete this book in time. Thank you all and I hope to see you all soon.

# ABOUT THE AUTHOR

Dear Fabulous Reader,

Thank you for reading. If you're a fan of Sam Wick, spread the word to friends, family, book clubs, and reader groups online.

*I would love to hear from you. Let's connect @*
*www.thechaseaustin.com*
*chaseaustincreative@gmail.com*

*Join my Facebook group below to get behind the scene content or follow me on Goodreads, Instagram or BookBub.*